RULES OF ENGAGEMENT

Make Me A Match Series

KAY LYONS

Kindred Spirits Publishing

____

Chapter 1

____

Wedding planner Eliza Bellefonte smiled at the happy couple and watched as they made their way onto the dance floor inside the tent dominating the rear of the seaside hotel.

Beneath the crisp white canvas, three hundred natural bamboo chairs with pearly-white cushions matched white-draped tables glittering like sea glass beneath the ten thousand artfully draped lights overhead.

Sand-colored runners ran the length of the long tables, and fairy lights twinkled with perfect randomness amid white and teal ribbon and green-ery. Intertwined with that was a mix of white hydrangeas and jasmine, the abundance of blooms dotted with crystals. Crystal and candles finished the table arrangements, the varying heights of the pillars lending even more elegance to the overall look.

The very young, very spoiled bride had insisted on beige and white for the foundation to make it more "beachy" even though she'd also demanded the tent have a floor to keep all that awful sand contained. Eliza remembered hearing that request —the hundredth or so at that point—and biting her inner lip to keep the smile pinned to her face.

Why bother with a beach wedding if sand wasn't a welcome guest?

But the bride was always right, even if she was neurotic about sand.

On the beach.

Be thankful, she mused, blinking her tired eyes. Six months ago she'd wondered if she'd have to close what was left of her business and file for bankruptcy due to the damage done when her partner— and boyfriend—had not only ended their relationship but taken off with half of the business as well as their administrative assistant. The two had secretly started their own company on the sly *before* Eliza realized what was happening and managed to charm clients into choosing them, then proceeded to rub Eliza's nose in the mud with every client they'd lured away.

Eliza forced her thoughts from the past and back on the couple of the day, focusing on the cashier's check currently processing its way into her account via her bank's phone app. One must never be too cautious, and this bridezilla had made Eliza a little too nervous with some of her last-minute demands. The changes always came with a comment about not paying if her wedding wasn't "just right."

The one ace up Eliza's sleeve was that the bride and Eliza's former assistant had bad blood between them, also over an old boyfriend, so the bride couldn't push too far or else she would risk having to hire her nemesis.

Still, she hadn't made Eliza's life any easier, because she'd known Eliza needed the business. And while Eliza had contracts in place to cover her own interests, the last thing she needed was negative social media.

Or another attorney fee.

There had been enough of both during her breakup with James and the business breakdown. So much so she'd had to get an attorney involved to protect herself. Now her newly named Dream Weddings was once again hers and hers alone.

But until she got her business back on its feet, it paid to be overly cautious—and overly accommodating. Because in the end, none of it mattered so long as she got paid.

"Gorgeous," Marsali Jones said. "As always."

Eliza turned to find her best friend of the last fourteen years standing behind her, another woman at Marsali's side. "Hey," she said with a smile after muting the mic she wore, which connected her to several of the catering staff. Eliza leaned into Marsali's quick hug and relished the embrace. "It's so good to see you. I've missed you."

"Right back at you," Marsali said, squeezing Eliza.

"I didn't see your name on the list."

Given that Marsali was a professional matchmaker and friends with Hollywood A-lister Oliver Beck, it wasn't unusual for Marsali to appear at functions hosting members of Wilmywood's movie production crowds. Bridezilla's father was part of Wilmington's movie-making group but—

"I'm Amelia's plus one," Marsali said, introducing Eliza to Amelia Porter, a set designer.

Amelia had sandy-brown hair pulled back in a simple twist, and wore a sleeveless rose-gold gown.

"When she said you guys were playing phone tag and her fiancé couldn't make it, I volunteered to come and convince you to pull off a mini-miracle for them," Marsali said, sliding Eliza a glance.

Oh, yeah. *That's* why Amelia's name had sounded familiar. "Ah, now I remember," Eliza said with a nod. "I'm sorry for the delay. As you can see, I've been a little busy, but I'd planned to try again first thing Monday." Eliza waved a hand at the interior and crowd. "When's the date?"

Amelia exchanged a glance with Marsali before making eye contact with Eliza.

"Two weeks," the woman said, wincing appropriately. "I *know*. It's asking a lot because it's a huge rush, but if I want a wedding instead of just a date at the courthouse, it's the only way. I'm… kind of on a time schedule and we don't want to take a year to plan something. But we want small and intimate, but special," she added, "since it's my first and only."

Eliza ignored the *first and only* comment and focused on the schedule. Two weeks? Eliza glanced at Marsali, noting her curly-headed friend had embraced her curls for the night. Marsali's hair was a thing of beauty but tended to have a life of its own some days. *Kind of like the craziness of her business*, she mused.

"You and I both know you can totally pull it off. *And*," Marsali added, "they'll happily pay you whatever it takes to make it happen in that time frame."

Marsali knew all of Eliza's secrets, including the time Bobby Jones had felt her up on the school bus, but more importantly, Marsali knew of her financial struggle to stay afloat since the big showdown with James.

"After seeing how amazing this is, I really want you to plan it, Eliza," Amelia said, her soft green eyes pleading. "Please. Say yes. I want a beautiful wedding, but there's no way I can do it all on my own."

Eliza stared out at the large area scattered with creamy lounges and love seats carefully placed in front of flowered backdrops. Outside, tulle billowed in the breeze, looped across the custom arch and decorated with gigantic flower arrangements. All of which had been ordered months in advance and carefully tracked.

Like Amelia, so many wanted the picture-perfect wedding but had no clue of the effort it took to make such things happen. The venue, lighting, seating, props, gowns, catering, band, staff, fittings, setup and take-down labor. The list was nearly endless, and no matter how simple a bride *said* they wanted a wedding to be, it always, *always* turned into more.

Weddings were a production, and depending on how deep the pockets the bride and groom—or their parents—had, the bigger and more elaborate things tended to get. But Eliza had yet to fail her clients. Whatever they wanted, they got, especially now when she worked so hard to showcase her talents over her competitors'.

After all, happy customers fueled her bank account and the safety those numbers gave her state of mind. Facing bankruptcy tended to make a person need that safety.

"Eliza?" Marsali gently nudged her arm. "I'll help however I can. I know it's late notice but… I'd consider it a personal favor. They've got a *great* story, and it deserves a celebration the likes of which only you can pull off. Please?"

Eliza shot both women a glance before she inhaled and opened the book she carried everywhere with her. She had copies of her copies, because when she couldn't find something digitally, she always fell back on her trusty paper bible of wedding information. "Two weeks," she murmured. "What day?"

"A weekend would be best but… any evening. You make it work," Amelia said. "And we'll make it work, too."

Wow. Now that was an unusual statement. Usually the bride had one date in mind and refused to budge from it, demanding the world stop whirling and shift around her date accordingly. But due to her change in business status… "You're in luck," she said, staring at the date that had brought her so much pain. "I have that Saturday open two weeks from now."

Because the very elaborate, very lucrative, very posh wedding she'd planned inside of Landfall had gone to James and his bimbo after James had finagled a golf game with the bride's father.

"Ink us in," Amelia said with a happy smile, her hands clasped in front of her like she wanted to dance and was trying to contain her excitement.

"Ink, huh? We haven't discussed my fees," Eliza murmured.

"If you can do something like this on a small scale in that time frame? Ink," Amelia said, nodding her head to confirm her words while giving Eliza a steady look.

Yeah. This had taken fourteen months to plan. Two weeks? Sure, no problem. "Do you have your gown?"

"No."

"Venue?"

"Not yet."

"Color scheme?"

Eliza glanced up and found Amelia beginning to look a bit wild-eyed and panicked. A soft laugh left her chest, and Eliza shook her head and snapped the book closed. She really needed to investigate panicked-bride hazard pay. "Can you meet me after the reception is over to give me an idea of what you'd like?"

"Absolutely. Does that mean you'll do it?" Amelia said.

Eliza agreed with a nod, rattled off the Saturday date just to confirm it, and Amelia gave Eliza a quick hug in response.

"Thank you. Thank you *so* much. Oh, I see someone I know and I have to go share the news. I'm so excited! Excuse me."

Marsali remained after Amelia hurried away, and once the woman was out of hearing range, Eliza stared up at her taller friend and lifted a single eyebrow high. "Are you trying to put me in an early grave?"

Marsali laughed and wrapped an arm around Eliza's shoulders, squeezing.

"I'm trying to show you that there are actually special couples out there who have the forever kind of love and Amelia and Lincoln are one of them."

"Uh-huh."

Marsali released Eliza and stepped in front of her to get her full attention.

"You amaze me. *How* do you make a living planning weddings that look like something out of a fairy tale or catalog shoot when you say you don't believe in love?"

"Easy. It's called a creative mind and financial security."

"Lizzie, you sound so jaded."

"And you know why."

"You can't let James destroy you."

"It's not just James and you know it. James was… James was just the icing on the proverbial wedding cake."

"Fine. Your parents' marriage was pretty awful."

"As was everyone else's in my family."

"I know, but that doesn't mean—"

"Maybe it does. Ever think of that? I'm sorry, but *I think* you're delusional, Miss Matchmaker. These two?" she said, lowering her voice to a cautious whisper. "I give them six months and *that's* being generous."

"Eliza. That's awful."

"Hey, I've been doing this since I was sixteen with my first job as an event assistant. The rose-colored glasses have long since shattered, especially after all I've been through this past year. I've learned the signs, and trust me, they don't have it."

"What signs?"

"For one, he's twice her age."

"Sometimes those work."

"And *sometimes* they're because Flirty Child Bride broke up the first marriage. He was also in the bar last night with his hands all over a—"

"No need to continue," Marsali interrupted, lifting her hand toward Eliza. "I like my naive state where I can still believe in love. Don't ruin it for me."

Eliza chuckled at her sweet friend's expression and hooked their arms, tugging Marsali toward the bar. "That's because you're in love with love. And a Hollywood hottie."

"Stop it. I am not."

"Hmm. Lie to yourself if you like. Me? I see how you eye your *Ollie*."

"Shh. Keep your voice down," Marsali ordered, taking a quick glance around. "He has other friends here, you know."

"So you admit it?" Eliza asked.

"Absolutely not. Oliver is… a good friend. Who, I might add, lives in LA while I'm here. Besides that, he only sees me as Mac's little sister."

"Which is why Mac's little sister needs to focus on the release of her book in what? Three weeks?"

"Two. And thank you. But you're still cynical," Marsali muttered.

Eliza shifted her weight on her aching feet and wished once again the bride hadn't been so anti-sand. The hardwood floor wasn't nearly as forgiving, and she had several hours to go yet. "I'm realistic. Love gets most everyone to the altar, but it does nothing to keep them married. Or even in business together."

"That's called integrity—and commitment."

"No argument there."

"That's it. You're killing me. I am going to fix you up no matter how much you protest. I didn't like James because there were some red flags you chose to ignore."

Eliza flinched. "Ouch."

"You know it's true. And I'm not saying that to be cruel, but simply because you settled for less than you deserve," Marsali added.

"He... I..."

"Exactly. The right guy will never treat you the way James did, and I'm going to make it my mission to find a man who will make you realize that. From now on, you are going to let me match you."

Eliza stared up at her taller friend and shook her head wryly. After the devastating betrayal by James and watching her mother scrimp by between men and the financial support they offered, the last thing she ever wanted to do was fall in love and find herself vulnerable to a man again. "Wanna bet?"

Chapter 2

Carter Hayes left his house via his rear deck and headed next door. Mac's home stood between Carter's and his brother Lincoln's and, ever since Mac had moved in, had acted as the in-between for the three bachelors. Evening free time was usually spent hanging out with whomever was free.

Lincoln had a pool in his backyard that they all used, and Mac had made his recently purchased home his by hiring a professional landscaper to come and create a visual haven that included an outdoor patio with a big-screen and built-in kitchen, as well as a beautiful garden that extended down to the canal. Both men left Carter thinking he needed to up his game since his yard only held an assortment of Piper's toys.

"Hey. How was Piper's first week?" Mac asked.

Carter jogged up the stone steps to Mac's raised patio. "Good. She's getting back to her usual self."

"Did she get over her upset?"

He chuckled and nodded. "Yeah. I keep reminding her that they'll be home to visit soon and will hang out with her on video chat sometimes until then. She isn't happy but she's adjusting."

Lincoln's twins had left for college a week ago and were settling in, and Piper hated that her cousins hadn't been around for her first day of pre-K. Now that she was going to school like the "big kids," she wanted them to be around to acknowledge the fact.

"Where's she now?"

"Breanne recommended another friend of hers to babysit," he said, referring to his niece. "They're inside watching a movie."

"*Another* babysitter?"

Carter avoided eye contact. "Yeah. The, uh, last one didn't work out."

"What happened?"

"Don't ask."

Mac started chuckling and Carter glared at his friend. "It's not funny."

"Ah, but it is. Little Miss Hottie came on to you, didn't she? I saw her getting out of her convertible in her cheerleading uniform," he said with a shake of his head. "Jailbait in sneakers."

Carter swiped a hand over his face and rubbed hard. "That girl had *just* turned sixteen. If Piper *ever* —" He broke off, unsure of what he'd do other than lock his daughter up in her bedroom and not let her out until she was forty.

Some men would've accepted the babysitter's offer of letting him be her "fabulous first" without a care for the consequences. But having a daughter of his own *and* not wanting to go to prison for statutory rape, Carter had fired the girl on the spot. Thankfully he had a nanny cam in the main room of the house as well as in Piper's, so when the girl had gotten mouthy over her dismissal, he'd pointed out that he had proof nothing happened.

"It's that bad-boy look," Mac stated with a grin. "The muscles, Harley, and tats? You're the triple crown."

"Bite me. And give me one of those," he said, wagging his fingers for a bottle of water. He'd rather have a beer but these days it paid to have a clear head. Especially when teenage girls were in his house. Thankfully this one seemed a little more grounded, but only time would tell. And he still had to find yet another one to pick up the slack since girls that age tended to be busy and notoriously unreliable.

The thought brought on others he'd been pondering a lot lately. His construction business was doing well. He had a good crew working for him. Maybe instead of finding a babysitter, he should try promoting someone to foreman and take a step back from things? Work after-school hours from home the way Mac had started doing after his first wife's death? "Where's Linc?"

"His text said he had some things to do but he'd be over soon."

"Man, he's been working crazy hours trying to get a handle on things before he and Amelia get married," Carter said.

The thought of his brother's upcoming nuptials made Carter wonder if their nightly "guy" ritual would continue after Lincoln tied the knot or if their hang-out sessions would dwindle down to the two remaining bachelors. Time would tell. Until then… "Haven't seen Marsali around. How's she doing?"

Carter asked the question to get a rise out of Mac, and sure enough, the man drew back and glared at Carter with all the animosity of a friend with a hot sister.

"Watch yourself," Mac said, pointing a finger at Carter.

"Just asking."

"Don't."

"Gentlemen," Lincoln said. "What are we arguing about tonight?"

Lincoln had managed to leave his house and join them without either of them noticing. "Marsali."

"Carter's underage babysitter and how he fired her."

Carter grimaced and shook his head at his older

brother. The last thing he needed was Lincoln reverting to old times when he'd had reason to lecture as Carter's legal guardian, but at thirty-three, he was a grown man and Lincoln had lost the right.

"Another one?" Lincoln asked.

"Had to be done. And I already hired another. Piper's checking her out tonight," Carter said, shooting a death glare at a smirking Mac.

"Good. But lay off Marsali. She isn't your type," Lincoln added.

"Definitely not," Mac said.

"How do you figure that? She's beautiful, smart, has her own business." Carter waited for the fallout.

"*No*," Lincoln and Mac said in unison.

"Why not? *She's* age appropriate," he said, just to egg them on. He really wasn't interested in Marsali, though his thoughts about her hotness were totally accurate. She was just a little too... sweet for him, though. And there was the fact she was his buddy's little sis. Even he knew not to cross that bridge. Do that, and if things go south, you lose the relationship *and* the friend. "You always say I look in the wrong places, which is why I hook up with the wrong women. Maybe Marsali and I—"

"Do you want me to kill you?" Mac demanded. "Keep talking."

Carter settled himself more comfortably in his seat so he could prop his foot on the coffee table.

"Guys, Piper needs a mama. How many times have you said I don't choose the best women?"

"Barflies would seldom be the right choice," Lincoln said. "And that's usually where you look."

"Which is why Marsali—"

"Where's Amelia?" Mac asked, ending the conversation.

"She is at a wedding for an associate," Lincoln said. "She wanted me to go but I had a ton of work to get done. But Marsali recommended a wedding planner, and the woman has proven hard to get in touch with, so they're going to track her down there."

"Eliza?" Mac asked, his eyebrows drawn down in a frown.

"Yeah, that's her," Lincoln said. "She planned the wedding taking place tonight."

"Wedding planner, huh? No justice of the peace?" Carter asked, knowing his brother wasn't the kind of guy who liked a big fuss.

"It might be my second but it's Amelia's first," Lincoln said with a shrug. "I want her to plan whatever she wants."

"Eliza's good," Mac said. "If anyone can put something together fast and keep it looking nice, she's the one. It'll help her out, too. She's had a rough year."

When Lincoln and Carter both stared at Mac, the man shrugged.

"Eliza's boyfriend was also her business partner.

He bailed after banging the secretary and then went into business with her, taking more than his share of clients with him through some underhanded deals."

"Nice guy," Carter said, wincing at the news. No one liked being betrayed, and having been through that type of scenario more than once himself, he empathized.

Lincoln's phone bleeped and Carter watched as his brother read the message and smiled.

"What? Amelia sexting you?" Carter asked.

"No, but the girls apparently stayed after the reception to talk wedding details and finished off some champagne. Amelia needs a ride."

"As does my sister," Mac said, shaking his head while staring at his smart watch. "Apparently we're their Ubers."

"Well, I'm due some entertainment," Carter said, standing when they did. "I'll tag along. Piper's babysitter is good for another two hours."

Mac didn't budge and Carter was aware of his friend staring at him. "What?" he asked. "Afraid I'm going to mack on your drunk sister?"

Lincoln groaned and Mac took a step closer, a dark glower on his face. Carter sighed. "Oh, come on. I'm not into Marsali, okay? She's cute but Linc's right. She's too sweet for my tastes. I'm just going along for kicks."

Mac's gaze narrowed, but after a moment, he seemed to accept Carter's words as truth, and the three of them made their way through their respective houses to properly lock up and inform before meeting outside of Mac's to climb into his large SUV.

Getting to the hotel didn't take long, and as they entered the lobby, feminine laughter filled the atrium. Carter spotted the ladies immediately, his gaze zeroing in on the dark-haired beauty sitting with Marsali and Amelia. The woman's bodacious smile drew his attention, and once he was close enough to get a better look, he noted how her deep green eyes sparkled with amusement. Pair those eyes with her sable hair and flushed cheeks, and she was the ultimate southern girl.

"Ah, there's my handsome man now," Amelia said, giggling. "Hi, future husband."

Lincoln bent over the couch where Amelia sat and bussed a kiss over her lips. Carter watched the exchange, a tug of envy tightening his muscles.

For all the talk and bluster and teasing, he envied the love Lincoln had found with Amelia. The high school sweethearts had parted ways back then but, twenty years later, were happier than he'd ever seen them.

His brother had been blessed twice over with quality women, whereas Carter had repeatedly chosen badly and ended up alone and struggling as a single dad.

Truth be told, he wanted what Lincoln had found, but after two tries, that didn't seem to be in the cards for him.

"Ahh, the bachelors," Marsali said, giving them a quizzical look along with a tilt of her curly head. "You know, it reflects poorly on me that my own brother won't let me match him up," she said. "Or *you*," Marsali said, pointing at Carter and waggling her finger. "You need to hire me. See how well I do?" she said, waving a hand toward the couple now snuggled up in the oversized chair where Amelia sat.

"I'll find my own match," Mac said to his sister. "And stop harassing my friends for clients."

"That's what I said," the brunette agreed with a nod of her finger-mussed hair and lift of her glass.

Mac chuckled. "Eliza, you're looking… happy."

"That's 'cause the check didn't bounce and Bridezilla's daddy was so happy to get her off his hands he gave us *that* to celebrate," Eliza said, waving a manicured hand toward a huge bottle of Dom sitting on the coffee table across from her. "Oh! And Amelia and I made some progress in planning her two-week wedding."

Cheers went up among the women once more, and they raised their glasses and downed the last of their drinks like sorority girls. The guys watched with varying degrees of amusement and head-shaking.

"Ladies, it's been fun but I have had a looong, exhausting day," Eliza said. "Amelia, I'll email you the contract sometime tomorrow evening."

"Thank you again," Amelia said. "I'm so glad you agreed to be our planner."

"Yes, thank you," Lincoln said to Eliza.

"You got it," Eliza said. "Marsali, girl, we need to stop saying we'll get together for that girls' weekend and actually do it."

"Agreed."

"Hold up," Mac said. "Eliza, how are you getting home?"

"Not going," Eliza stated, setting her glass on the table. "Perks of being a wedding planner. I get a room and a write-off when an event ends after a certain time. I just have to get to my room and remember not to skinny-dip in the hot tub on the way," she said, scooting to the edge of the couch cushion.

Skinny-dip? Carter mused. He wouldn't mind seeing that.

Eliza got to her feet and wobbled, and standing closest to her, Carter quickly reached out to steady her.

"Hmm. Hello. Who are you again?"

Amelia introduced them and Carter ignored Mac's glare. His buddy couldn't claim "off-limits" on both his sister *and* her beautiful friend. That just wasn't cool. "Nice to meet you, Eliza," he said, sliding her arm through his. "How about I walk you to your room?"

Chapter 3

Eliza stared up into the slate-colored eyes of Carter Hayes and wondered if her anti-men stance wasn't just a little too hasty. Because right now? Looking at him? Carter Hayes checked the boxes with his tall, muscular frame and angular face.

His good looks had that bad-boy slant she'd *always* found so appealing, the one that made her lose her senses and do stupid things like catch feelings and fall in love—until said bad boys lived up to their reputations and she was left with a broken heart.

"Eliza?"

Her name emerged in that deep, husky voice of his, and like it or not, a shiver ran the length of her spine before she mentally stomped on it like an annoying bug. "Mm?"

Carter chuckled at her response and even *that* sounded sexy.

Yup. She was officially drunk—well, *tipsy* might be a better word, but she was definitely something to be considering him as anything other than trouble.

Obviously champagne bubbles held more punch than she'd thought.

Maybe it's the fact you haven't eaten since breakfast?

Regardless, the next time she saw Carter Hayes, he wasn't as likely to be so handsome.

Yeah, right.

"I'm going to walk Eliza past the hot tub to her room. I'll meet you back here in a bit," Carter said.

She smiled at his joke and earned another grin from him.

"Behave yourself," Mac said, the word a low growl.

Eliza giggled and then frowned at her reaction, both to the handsome stranger and Mac's perturbed expressions.

Please. She so didn't sleep with people she'd just met. Or skinny-dip with them.

She lifted a hand to wave goodbye at her friends, ignoring Marsali's exaggerated wink and wide smile.

Eliza turned toward the bank of elevators on the left. Except… that was a half wall with dining tables on the other side.

When had they moved the elevators? She would've thought it would take longer than a day, and they'd been right there this morning.

"This way, sweetheart."

Sweetheart? She was nobody's sweetheart. Or darling. Or honey. She'd worked her tail off to get her business off the ground, and then *stupidity* had walked away with half of it—and her administrative assistant.

Her mood darkened like it did every time she thought of the betrayal, and she leaned into the hard, solid body steadying her as well as steering her toward the right. She allowed Carter to lead since he seemed to know where the elevators had been moved.

Which begged the question of *why* he knew. She knew the layout of every nice hotel in town due to her profession but he... Why did he know?

She peeked up at him from beneath her lashes. "Do you do this often?"

"What?"

"Walk strange women to their hotel rooms. I mean, I'm not *strange* but... You know what I mean."

His lips quirked up at the corners and brought out a dimple.

Seriously? Could the man be any more gorgeous?

She squinted. Hard. Waiting to find some flaw in him, because there had to be *one*.

Looks-wise he passed muster and then some, but maybe he had some unsightly rash? STD? Wore nipple rings? Because that was *so* not attractive. Or maybe—

"Do you do this often? Get drunk in hotel lobbies?"

A giggle burst out of her at the ludicrous suggestion, and she winced at the sound, knowing no professional wedding planner should be caught drunk-giggling. Ever. "No. I rarely get to kick back with the girls, but the Dom was a nice surprise bonus from Bridezilla's daddy, and with another wedding tomorrow, I knew better than to drink it all. Plus, we had Amelia's wedding to plan so... Sharing was the proper thing to do."

"I see. So tell me, Eliza, why haven't I met you before?" he asked. "I've known Mac a few months now and Marsali hangs out sometimes but... I haven't seen you around."

"Summer is my busiest season. I keep meaning to stop by and see Mac's new house but there just hasn't been time. Plus, Mac and I don't hang out unless Marsali is around."

"Why's that?"

Color surged to her face and she felt it burn. "It's... awkward."

"You can tell me."

"Well, he, um, kissed me about a year ago."

"It wasn't a good kiss?"

"Like kissing my brother."

Carter's booming laughter filled the hotel lobby.

"Brother, huh?" he said, flashing her another sexy smile.

Did he actually look pleased at the news?

The kiss had been an accident. She and Mac had met by happenstance in downtown Wilmington and chatted briefly. Upon saying goodbye, he'd leaned down to hug her right as she'd risen into him, and she'd slipped on a rock beneath her shoe, meshing their mouths instead. Mac had apparently thought she was actually *kissing* him and taken it a step further until she'd pulled away. Much eye contact was avoided because of her horrified response.

Which was why there was no need to share that information with anyone. Much less Mac's neighbor.

Too late now.

As they crossed the expansive lobby, Eliza realized she should feel nervous about having a big, hunky stranger walk her to her door, but given that Marsali and Amelia waited below, not to mention Mac, she felt perfectly safe. One yelp and her friends would come running, especially in the open atrium design of the hotel, where sound tended to carry.

"What floor?" he asked.

The elevator doors opened just as they arrived, and once the passengers got off, Carter urged her inside. Eliza turned too quickly, and her brain slushed among the bubbles that had made their way there and bobbed like a buoy as a result. "Ohh," she said, her body gently banging into the elevator wall. "Head rush."

Carter lifted an eyebrow at her and chuckled again.

"You're a cute drunk, I'll give you that."

"I'm not drunk."

"No?"

"Nope," she said, making a popping sound on the P.

His gaze shifted downward in the general direction of her mouth because of what she'd done, and she was glad the wall had her back with the trail of heat left behind as a result. All from those eyes of his. And, well, the rest of him, too.

Who knew a dark gaze and sooty lashes could be such a thing for her? Until now she'd never really thought she had a preference for eye color. Turned out she did.

And, okay, maybe she was a little more *tipsy* than she'd first thought while sitting on the couch, because the floor did seem to be tilting just a bit— but it was only because she hadn't eaten since breakfast.

What were they talking about?

Oh, yeah. "Two glasses of champagne does not make me drunk."

"Is that right?"

"It's because I didn't eat," she said defensively. "The wedding today was a huge pain in the—" She forced herself to stop and licked her dry lips, closing her eyes and pasting on what she hoped was a professional demeanor. "Well, let's just say the bride today was difficult," she said. And until she managed to get her business back up to speed, she couldn't afford to hire a full-time assistant, which left her hiring untrained hourlies who had to be constantly watched and instructed and that meant… not having time to eat.

"What floor, sweetheart?"

"Four. No, wait. Six. I'm on six."

"You're sure?"

That look of his… Did the man know the power he wielded with that face? The amusement in his gaze left her lifting her chin high. "I was on the fourth floor *first*, but there was an issue with the room and they switched me, so yup."

Crap, she did it again. She looked away from the gaze that was once more on her mouth and watched as he stretched out a long arm toward the numbered panel. From there her gaze slid up his arm to what she could see of his tattoo. She'd always had a thing for tats, too. Especially on muscles that looked good enough to—

"Something on your mind?" he asked.

"N-no."

"You're staring."

"You're… very tan," she mused, scrambling for an excuse.

Carter pressed the button and then settled his

lean hips against the elevator wall opposite hers. The stance should've looked slouchy, but instead he looked relaxed and amused and *tan*, and it made her think of some naughty things to do while the elevator climbed.

"I work construction. Comes with the territory."

"The muscles must be part of the job, too, then." The words left her mouth before she could stop them, and she silently berated herself for the nervousness making her say—and *think*— things she shouldn't.

Carter tucked his chin toward his chest, his gaze narrowed on her, and crossed his arms over his chest. The move made his biceps bulge and stretch the seams of his sea-blue shirt, revealing more of the tattoos. She blinked at the sight and tried to unglue her tongue from the roof of her mouth.

"Does that make part of your job looking as beautiful as the bride?"

The line was kind of cheesy, but there was an appreciation in his gaze that left her believing his words to be sincere. *Or that of a bad boy trying to get laid?* "Are you always this flirty with women you don't know?"

"Only when I'm interested."

She rolled her eyes and shook her head with an uncomfortable laugh. "Well, I'm *not* interested," she said, throwing his choice of words back at him.

"Why not?"

"What, hasn't a woman ever said no to you?"

"I get the feeling you're saying no for the wrong reasons," he said, ignoring her question.

Wrong reasons? Oh, she had *all* the right reasons. "Relationships muck things up," she said, reminding herself, aloud, while staring at his gorgeousness. "And I don't do one-night stands."

No matter how tired she was. No matter how much she'd like to be cradled against Carter's broad chest, held in those tatted arms, if only for a moment.

"Good to know. But what things?"

What?

Oh, *things*. Like friendship things. Relationship things. *Business* things. "*Every*thing."

"How so?"

She shoved her hair out of her face. "People fall in love and trust people and then… it doesn't work. Take today for example. Bridezilla, for all her faults, seems to be in love. Whereas the groom propositioned me before *and* after the wedding." The jerk had even offered to throw in a "bonus" if she'd agree.

"All men don't cheat, sweetheart."

She blinked, drawn to his words and the sexy tone used to say them.

Thankfully the doors opened with a musical chime, and she shoved herself off the elevator wall but then tripped exiting into the hallway.

Carter caught her from behind and kept her from taking a nosedive into the floor. The crazy carpet pattern and colors beneath her feet swirled like a sick carnival ride.

But him holding her? Those muscled arms wrapped around her as he helped her straighten?

She turned and wound up pressed against his equally muscled chest and held on to those tattooed arms for dear life until the world stopped spinning. "Thanks," she mumbled. "Th-that wasn't from drinking."

"Uh-huh."

"Really. I can be clumsy. It's a fact."

He smiled again and her stomach did a somersault.

"Sure it wasn't the shock of what I said?"

"Men say that, then they do what they want anyway."

As fast as he'd caught her and saved her from the fall, Carter released her to keep the elevator doors from closing behind him. She watched as he swiped her purse up off the elevator floor and handed it over before he wrapped his arm around her shoulders.

"You obviously haven't met the right man."

The right man? Meaning him?

Any woman in her right mind would steer clear of someone like Carter, if for no other reason than the fact women would be *constantly* throwing them-selves at him and eventually… Well, what were the odds he'd always say no? "I'm a realist," she said dryly.

"You believe everyone cheats?"

"I don't want to argue with you." Her entire body ached with fatigue, and her cool bedsheets called her name.

"We're not arguing. We're discussing. So tell me. Have *you* ever cheated in a relationship?"

"What? No!" She glanced up at him and found him looking curiously… relieved?

"No?"

"No," she repeated, lifting her chin. "Absolutely not."

"Well, neither have I, sweetheart. When I'm with someone, I'm theirs. Which," he added, "proves your theory wrong."

She was still stumbling over the thought of him being… well, hers. "Fine. Maybe not *everyone* cheats. But the odds? Not good. Because maybe they haven't because they haven't been together long enough, or they haven't had the opportunity… but they want to."

"That's a little dark."

"Yeah, well, I've planned many a vow renewal ceremony for couples trying to repair a marriage after cheating. And that's just the ones who get caught. I'm sure there are plenty of people out there who've cheated and managed to get away with it."

"Okay, then."

Uh-huh. Pretty Boy wasn't loading up the charm now. Not after that rant. Score one for the cynic! "See? I win." A laugh bubbled out of her before she shrugged, unapologetic. "Marsali says I'm jaded."

"Marsali seems to be right in your case. But I'd hardly call that a win. I think you just haven't met the right guy. Because *that guy* would never give you reason to doubt your relationship."

"Doesn't matter at this point. I'm done. Done, done, done."

Carter stared down at her with an expression she couldn't quite pinpoint, and she looked away and busied herself by opening her bag to try to find her key card.

"Need some help?"

She dug around inside the abyss with no luck. After waiting patiently for several long moments, Carter held out his hand in a silent offer to take a look. She normally wouldn't hand her bag to a stranger, but her head was starting to pound from the champagne and hunger, and she felt exhaustion creeping into the very depths of her soul.

The topic of conversation sucked, too, because she knew she was a little bitter *and* jaded, but if anyone had walked in her shoes, they would be, too. She saw the best and worst of the couples who hired her, as well as their families and friends.

She let Carter have the carry-all that served as her purse, and after a poking around several seconds, he produced the lost key card still inside the paper case with her room number. Thank goodness she didn't have to try to remember it. "Yay," she said softly, cheering in her relief, because the last thing she wanted was to have to go back to the lobby to the front desk and get another.

Carter smiled that sexy smile of his that had no doubt lured many a woman to do bad, *bad* things, but before he gave her back the bag, he pulled something else from the depths and held up one of her business cards. She watched as he tucked it into his pocket. "What are you doing?"

"Getting your number."

"Why?"

"Because I want it."

He gave her back the tote and took her hand in his, and she couldn't help but think how big and strong and masculine his palm felt as he tugged her along the hallway. "Are you going to post a bad review?"

"No."

"Recommend me to an engaged couple?"

"Don't know any other than Lincoln and Amelia."

Then why take her card? She pondered the possibilities and glanced around, frowning at the numbers posted at the beginning of various hallways. "We're lost," she said. "I think my room is the other way."

"It's this way," Carter countered without pausing. "So what's his name?"

"Whose name?"

"The man who left you so jaded you don't believe in love."

"Shhhhh," she said, digging in her heels and forcing him to stop. "It's not marketab-ble to be a wedding planner who doesn't believe in *love*." She shook her hand loose from his to lift it, pinky raised, toward him. "You can't tell *any*one. I mean it. Promise."

Carter looked like he was torn between laughter and disbelief, but he dutifully lifted his hand and pinky swore to keep her bitterness to himself.

"Eliza… can I tell *you* a secret?"

"I s'pose." Oh, her head felt *really* fuzzy. Maybe she shouldn't have downed the last of her champagne before leaving the lobby.

Eliza tried to pull her hand away again, but his finger tightened over hers. Carter used his hold to gently tug her closer, and he leaned low, until his lips were near her ear.

"I don't like it that you don't believe in love."

"You… don't?"

That smile. This one made her tired toes curl in her comfortable flats and, dang, it made her want to be one of those women who did bad things. To him. With him. Had he always smelled so *good*?

"Hey? Eliza?"

She blinked up at him and found his gaze narrowed on her again, even though the hallway spun around them like those shots they did in the movies that always made her look away before she lost her popcorn and cherry Twizzlers. "Yeah?"

"You still with me, sweetheart?"

"I need to lie down."

"Come on, sweetheart. Let's get to your room before you pass out on me."

Her room. She couldn't wait to lie down.

And yet… her bed was big and cold and *empty*.

Maybe she should get a dog? Then she'd at least have someone to sleep with who wouldn't cheat on her. Someone loyal and loving and always happy to see her when she got home. "Doodles are cute."

"Pardon?"

"I need a dog."

His expression sharpened at her statement and the change in subject, and he urged her a little faster down the hall.

Finally they made it to the door of her room, and she watched as he swiped the plastic over the pad and the door unlocked with a flash of green and three short beeps.

Carter pushed the door open and held it with his foot, gently ushering her inside, where she leaned against the closest wall for support.

"Here's your key card. Don't forget to lock the door behind me."

"I won't," she mumbled, forcing her tired lashes up to meet his gaze. "I'm sorry."

"For what, sweetheart?"

"Just... forget everything I've said, okay? I'm... *really* hungry."

She felt his hand brush her hair back from her face, and the moment he touched her skin, she forgot how to breathe.

"You're asleep on your feet, aren't you?"

"She was an *awful* bride. And James keeps hiring my staff out from under me and... she was *awful*."

Carter's thumb drifted over her cheek, her lower lip. The pad felt a bit rough, sandpapery, but once again he left a trail of fire behind. And the look on his face, his eyes...

"Sweet dreams, Eliza."

"Wait. Wh-what are you going to dream about?"

Carter chuckled, and oh, that sound. It was low and sexy and it rolled over her skin and enveloped her like a warm blanket and a back rub combined. The kind that always led to more.

"You. Definitely you, sweetheart. Now lock the door behind me. I'll be in touch."

"No, no, wait," she said, forcing herself to focus with a brain-rattling shake of her head. She didn't want this to be his impression of her. This tired, tipsy, let-him-touch-her-and-say... Or to *think*... "I want my business card."

He backed into the hallway and gave her that toe-curling grin again as the door began to swing closed. "Nope," he said, emphasizing the *P* just before it shut.

Chapter 4

The following day, Carter squinted across the expanse of the beach and wished he had a pair of binoculars to see whether or not the woman who'd caught his attention fifteen or twenty minutes ago was Eliza Bellefonte.

It looked like her, but from this distance, he just couldn't be sure.

"Daddy!"

Piper drew his attention, and he followed her pointing finger toward the dolphins breaking the surface of the Atlantic. "Cool. How many do you see?"

"Three!"

He chuckled at her excitement. "Are you sure you don't want a dolphin birthday party instead of mermaid?"

His adorable imp turned her back to the surf

and placed both hands on her slim hips, lifting her chin high.

"I'm Ariel, Daddy. See?"

The last was said with a lift of her hands, palms to the sky, to indicate her blazing red hair, and there was so much attitude and sass in the statement that he couldn't help but chuckle. "So I see. Promise me something, kiddo."

"What, Daddy?"

"Promise me that when you're a teenager, you'll turn down the boys and still go on Daddy-daughter dates with me."

She grinned at him, flashing her dimples, and nodded. "Of course!"

Piper went back to building a mermaid army on the sand with a plastic mold, and Carter found himself glancing toward the hotel farther down the beach once more. "Hey, you about ready to go get some food?"

"Ice cream?"

"I never should've let you talk me into that," he said with a wry shake of his head.

"It's only on Daddy-daughter Day, Daddy."

True. Dessert first once a week wasn't *that* bad of a thing, was it? Especially when she ate well the rest of the time. "So what's the answer? You getting hungry?"

"Yeah."

"Let's get moving then."

"Okay." Piper scrambled to her feet, and he

held out the easy-on sundress she wore as a cover. Once dressed, she wriggled her tiny, freckled toes into her flip-flops, and he smiled at the mix of sand and the blue nail polish the last babysitter had applied.

They left their chairs and lowered umbrella behind and headed in the direction of the hotel and the indoor-outdoor restaurant.

"Where are we going?"

"How does a big-girl restaurant sound for today?"

"Okay. But I get ice cream?"

"That's the deal." He squinted behind his dark sunglasses, but the woman had her back to them. If it was Eliza, she didn't look happy. She paced the beach in back of the hotel with a cell phone to her ear and some kind of notebook in hand.

He and Piper closed the distance, and confirmation that it was Eliza came as a kick to his gut, a fact that wasn't lost on him.

After walking her to her door last night, he'd spent the ride home and the rest of his waking hours pondering the beautiful mess that was Eliza Bellefonte.

From what he'd gleaned from Mac about her business partnership/personal relationship going bad, she'd been put through the wringer and was still recovering on a multitude of levels.

If he was smart, he'd leave things as they'd ended. Especially since she'd declared herself uninterested. But he remembered her humor and beauty and sweetness, and from thirty feet away, Carter shook his head at the man stupid enough to hurt her.

Hearts were fragile and not to be toyed with, and he had a daughter growing up in a world where people trashed other people without a care as to the consequences to their lives. He wasn't okay with that. And even if he and Eliza were never more than friends, he'd at least like her to see not all men were cheating losers.

He and Piper finally made it to the area behind the hotel and the woman occupying his thoughts. Eliza released a low sound of frustration and muttered to herself, a small foot stomping into the sand.

"Is there a problem?" he asked.

"Oh!"

Eliza swung to face them, looking casual yet professional in white knee-length shorts and a blue sleeveless blouse, dark sunglasses on her nose. Her bag and sandals were tossed aside nearby.

He took in Eliza's pinched features and the firm line of her mouth and still felt the same pull he had last night.

"Hi, I'm Piper," his daughter said. "What's your name?"

Eliza seemed to notice his daughter for the first time. She managed a smile.

"I'm Eliza. It's nice to meet you, Piper."

"What's going on?" he asked, eyeing the wood pieces scattered on the sand. Another glance revealed plastic standup signs stating that the area was closed for a private event.

"I'm having… setup issues."

"Meaning?"

"The man who is supposed to be here putting this together right now didn't show and isn't coming," she said, voice laden with frustration.

"Maybe I can help you out."

"Oh, I couldn't… I mean—"

The phone in her hand bleeped, and she glanced at the face only to exhale in a rush.

"Okay. Well. That was my backup plan saying they're out of town."

"Eliza? Let me help."

He watched as she took a deep breath and came to terms with the fact she was out of options and going to have to accept the offer.

"Okay. Yeah, I'd… appreciate it. If the bride looks over her balcony and finds the arbor in pieces, I'm likely to have an even bigger problem on my hands."

"Okay. Where's the schematic?"

"Here, but… are you sure?"

"Yes. But I have to take Piper to the snack bar first."

"Oh. Of course. Unless…maybe I could do it? I'd be happy to, I mean."

She probably offered so he would get started on

the project, but in the scheme of things, it didn't matter. Both had to be done. "Yeah, sure. Thanks. Piper, Eliza is going to take you to get your ice cream while I be a good friend and help her by building this, okay?" he asked.

"Ice cream for *lunch*?" Eliza asked, looking appropriately shocked.

"Only on Daddy-daughter dates," Piper said. "Dessert first is a *rule*. Then I have to eat my food."

Eliza stared at him, lowering her voice. "This is your Daddy-daughter *date*?"

He could feel Eliza about to protest his involvement and recant her acceptance and hurried to stop it. "Go get the ice cream while I get started. And don't worry, she's going through a growth spurt, so she's always hungry. She'll eat despite the treat."

Eliza looked like she wanted to argue but was feeling that spot between a rock and hard place. He pulled cash from his pocket.

"Oh, please. No. I'll get it," Eliza said. "It's the least I can do since I'm taking time from your date."

He hesitated but then accepted the offer with a nod. "Piper? Only one scoop. Got it?"

"Got it."

"Have fun, ladies. I'll get to work on this. Piper, behave and mind your manners with Ms. Eliza, okay?"

"Okay, Daddy."

Piper grasped Eliza's hand and tugged her

toward the hotel, and Eliza glanced over her shoulder at him one last time before turning away.

Carter watched them go, enjoying the sway of Eliza's hips in her shorts before he finally forced himself to focus and got to work, glancing over the instructions quickly.

The arbor wouldn't take long to build, but getting it securely anchored in the sand so it wouldn't topple in the breeze during the ceremony would be the more difficult task. He wondered how she did this multiple times a week, but then remembered her help hadn't shown up.

Carter put together the long sides of the wooden structure before he worked on the more complicated top. Something made him glance up, and he spotted Piper a ways away, looking up at Eliza with a huge smile as they made their way toward him.

His heart tugged at the sight. His baby girl deserved to have a loving mother in her life, but the handful of women he'd dated since Piper's mother had split had been so self-involved they'd demanded they come first, something that didn't work for him as a single dad to an infant or toddler at the time.

He'd quickly learned few women were willing to take a backseat to a child even during the dating stage, and his relationships had never been more than casual since. His soon-to-be sister-in-law and niece would have to fill the void in Piper's life, at least for the time being, and instead of hiring a slew of babysitters, he'd decided to go ahead and promote someone within his business so that he could work after-school hours at home like Lincoln had when his first wife was killed. After all, it wasn't like he'd ever get these years with Piper back.

"Wow. You're moving right along," Eliza said once she was close enough for him to hear.

"Daddy, look. They had my favorite," Piper said.

"Thanks," he said to Eliza, lifting his chin toward his daughter.

"Of course."

He went back to work and noted the way Eliza immediately pitched in and acted as an assistant. Some people didn't work well enough together to build a cardboard puzzle, much less an arbor, but Eliza tried to stay a step ahead of him so that she was ready to hand him whatever the next piece or tool or fastener happened to be.

Nearby, Piper finished her ice cream and began making sand angels in the shade provided by the tall hotel.

"I hate that I've interrupted your day together," Eliza said. "But I'm so glad you were around to save the day. I don't know how I'll ever repay you."

"Dinner would be nice."

"Oh, of course. I'd be happy to pay for your Daddy-daughter dinner."

"Not what I had in mind," he said, fitting the top in place. "I mean dinner, just you and me."

"Oh. Um…"

"Come on, Eliza. Aren't you the tiniest bit curious about us?" He tightened the screw and noted the way she wouldn't look at him.

"Us? No."

"That was a little too quick, sweetheart. Makes me not believe you," he said, sliding her a look from behind his sunglasses. He sat kneeling on the sand in front of her and shoved his glasses atop his head so she could see his eyes, even if he couldn't see hers. "Give me a legitimate reason why you're so against a simple dinner."

"I'm… just not interested."

"Because of some loser who hurt you?"

"Because I don't have time to date."

"Eliza? Where do you want these?" a woman called, carrying a bucket of flowers.

Eliza looked toward the woman bearing a florist logo-ed T-shirt and waved a hand toward the right.

"There's fine. Thank you, Jess," Eliza said. "I have to go," she said to him. "I have a wedding to set up."

She'd shoved herself to her feet and had turned away when he said, "I'm not taking no for an answer."

Carter saw the other woman's eyebrows rise in curiosity as she glanced between the two of them, but Eliza didn't bother to look back.

"You're going to have to," she called over her shoulder.

He got to his feet, motioning toward one of the teenage boys who'd just lowered a bucket of flowers to the sand. "Hey, give me a hand here, would you? Grab that side."

"Dude, that was harsh," the kid said, laughing at Eliza's rejection as he joined Carter.

Carter never took his gaze off of Eliza and knew the moment she took a discreet glance his way. He winked at her and smiled when her lips parted in a visual gasp. "That it was," he said to the teenager.

But he still wasn't giving up.

Chapter 5

The following afternoon, Carter hefted his almost five-year-old daughter, Piper, higher against his chest and shoulder and buried his head in her stomach with a ferocious growl. Her little-girl giggles filled his ears and brought a squeeze to his heart as they always did.

Sometimes he wondered if Piper's mother ever had any regrets walking out on them the way she had, but then... he didn't want to find out. The last thing Piper needed was for her mom to appear and possibly reconnect, only to leave *again.*

"There you are," Amelia said, smiling from a chair on the deck surrounding Lincoln's pool. "Hi, Piper."

"Hiii. Daddy, stop tickling me," Piper said, still laughing.

"I only do it because redheads are my favorite

snack," he told Piper, letting her slide to the ground now that they'd arrived.

"No shoes?" Amelia asked.

"The monster ate them," Piper said quickly, glancing up at Carter with sweet yet conniving innocence.

"Happens a lot in our house," Carter said, making a fierce Dad face at his daughter. "But only to little girls who don't pick up after themselves and put their shoes in the bin where they go."

"I found one of 'em."

Carter chuckled and tousled his daughter's ponytailed head before he handed over the unicorn pool ring he'd also carried from his house.

Piper asked permission to get in and he nodded. She quickly yanked the unicorn float over her head and ran for the edge, jumping in like the little mermaid she was.

"You ladies are looking lovely. Where's Linc?" Carter asked.

"He had to take a real estate call, but he'll be back out in a minute," Amelia said. "And Mac is on his way over."

"So, Carter…" Marsali said from her chair.

Carter turned his head. "So, Marsali?"

The women both wore sunglasses but he saw the quick glance they exchanged. His gut tightened in warning because he knew what they were about to ask.

Maybe he should go check on Lincoln? Give Mac a hand with whatever he was doing?

Because despite the hours between Friday night and now, he still wasn't sure what he was going to do with that card he'd pulled from Eliza's purse.

"You and Eliza looked awfully good together," Marsali said. "I think my brother was a bit jealous."

Carter grinned unabashedly. "Yeah, well, Mac will get over it."

"Mac heard that."

Carter turned to find his neighbor closing the distance between Mac's house and Lincoln's, a beach towel thrown over his shoulder and a cooler in hand.

"And you'd better not do anything you'll regret," Mac continued as he made it to where Carter still stood.

"Why would I regret it?" Carter asked his friend.

Mac lifted his sunglasses from his face for a moment to shoot Carter a glare before lowering them again.

"Because I'd make you," Mac said, matter-of-fact. "Eliza's family."

"Ah, yeah, she mentioned you'd kissed her and it was like kissing her brother."

Mac shoved the cooler into Carter's belly for that low blow, and he grunted from it even as he grinned. Yeah… apparently Mac didn't feel *entirely* brotherly about Eliza.

"You *kissed* her?" Marsali asked, gasping. "*When*? *Why* didn't either of you tell me this? Oh, you wait until I talk to her again!"

Mac leaned his head back as though calling on every ounce of patience he could muster.

"It was a long time ago and because it was awkward and never happened again. Let's move on," Mac said, moving to toss his towel onto a lounger by the ladies before using two fingers to point to his eyes and then at Piper in that age-old *I'm eyeing you, kid* motion.

"Don't jump on me!" Piper screamed, kicking and splashing and laughing in an effort to get away from Mac to the opposite side of the pool.

"Yes, let's move on. So, Carter," Marsali said again. "I sensed some major chemistry between you and Eliza."

"Chemistry is important," Amelia said. "That's one of the questions on Marsali's dating list. Oh, I can't wait until your book releases in a few weeks! I'm going to buy copies for all my friends and have you sign them."

Carter set the cooler aside, kicked off his slides, and tossed the towels wrapped around his neck for carrying. "I have to swim with my kid."

"Nah, buddy. I've got her," Mac called from the pool, laughing. "You just enjoy the interrogation."

"Have you talked to Eliza since?" Marsali asked.

While Mac spouted his nonsense, Amelia ran

over and grasped Carter's arm, dragging him toward the loungers and away from the water.

"Sit. I'll get you a drink," Amelia said, pushing him down.

"Ladies—"

"Uh-uh. We need answers," Marsali said.

Carter stared at the beautiful faces looking back at him and barely suppressed the groan struggling to emerge. Mac's mocking laughter from the pool didn't help. Carter glanced toward his neighbor, spotting Mac's smug grin.

Brother, Carter mouthed, throwing Eliza's description of the kiss back at his friend.

Mac drew his arm back and sent it flying, and water sprayed from the pool, dousing the three of them. The ladies shrieked but this time Carter was the one smirking. Given the chemistry between him and Eliza, he could guarantee a kiss would feel anything but brotherly.

Amelia returned and pressed a cold drink into his hand. He popped the tab and tilted his head for a drink, gaze landing on both females as they turned sideways on the loungers to give him their full attention.

He lowered the can and sighed. "Have at it, ladies."

SEVERAL HOURS and coats of sunscreen on Piper's pale skin later, Carter peeked over to the umbrella-shaded chair where his baby girl sat eating watermelon. Pink marked both cheeks in a wide crescent while pink streams ran down her chin.

"I can't get over how beautiful she is," Amelia said. "If one of the casting reps were to ever see her—"

"No," he said instantly. "She is not going to be a show-business brat," he said, referring to Amelia's connections with Wilmington's Hollywood elite.

"Modeling?" she asked next.

"Forget it."

"Stop grumbling at my fiancée," Lincoln said from his position by the grill.

"I'll stop when your fiancée quits trying to corrupt my baby girl."

Amelia held up her hands in surrender. "I'm just saying she'd be perfect."

"Good news," Marsali said, leaving the house where she'd excused herself a bit ago. "She's coming."

Every adult head turned in Carter's direction. Seriously? "Who's coming?" he asked, playing dumb though his gut identified the mysterious visitor.

"Eliza," Marsali said with a shake of her damp curls. "I called to check on her and she said she's made some progress with the wedding prep for you guys," Marsali said to Amelia. "She, uh, mentioned not being able to read some of her notes from last night, so I told her we were just hanging out by the pool so… she's stopping by to get some details straightened out and get the signed contract from you."

"Wonderful," Amelia said, moving to Lincoln's side to give him a quick kiss in her excitement. "Won't be long now."

"Long enough," Lincoln said.

Carter watched the two lovebirds and tried to rid himself of the tug of envy. Maybe he was a softie, but he really did want that kind of connection with a woman someday. The lasting kind that might not be perfect but gave him the life he wanted for Piper and himself.

His problem was finding the right woman.

Especially when certain women declared themselves uninterested....

Chapter 6

That evening, Carter set the baby monitor on the coffee table and sat down beside his brother on Mac's newly decorated patio, staring out at the beautiful landscaping fronting the canal running in back of all three of their homes. Of the three yards, Mac's was by far the most elaborate with its designer lighting, domed gazebo, and sitting areas. "Where's Mac?"

"He was here earlier but took the bike somewhere to scope out a business."

Mac had his hand in a little of everything. Investments, chain stores, restaurants. When debating an investment, he liked to go as a customer to check out the management and staff before making a final decision.

Carter nodded, a tug of envy in his heart over his friend's two-wheeled adventure. He'd put his bike in storage the day after Piper had been born, determined not to take any chances when he had a kid to raise. His parents had been killed in a car accident, and while he was a safe biker, far too many motorcycle riders were taken down because of other drivers. "Where's Amelia?"

"She's meeting Eliza and Izzy for a dress fitting."

"On a Sunday?" he asked, glancing at his watch to note the time.

"Eliza pulled some strings to make it happen so Amelia could get the ball rolling."

"Good. That's cool. I, uh, saw Eliza yesterday," Carter said. "When Piper and I went to the beach."

"So I heard."

After the nonstop interrogation by the ladies, he wasn't surprised the news had traveled. "Yeah, one of Eliza's workers didn't show and wasn't there to put together an arbor for a wedding, so I helped her out."

Carter felt Lincoln's gaze boring a hole into him.

"Why do I get the feeling there's more to the story?"

Carter inhaled and sighed, wondering how his older brother always knew when he was holding back. Some kind of sixth sense? Considering Linc had been his guardian since Carter was thirteen, Carter would believe it. He'd certainly given Lincoln reason to be thorough in his questioning during those years. "I asked her out."

Lincoln sat forward in his chair.

"You demanded a date for payment?" his brother asked quietly.

"I didn't demand anything."

"You couldn't have just *helped* her out?"

Carter grimaced at the lecturing tone of Lincoln's voice. Amelia and Marsali had thought it romantic when he'd mentioned the asking to them. "I *did* help her out. She mentioned not knowing how to repay me so I—"

"Demanded a date," Lincoln growled. "Did you really think that would work?"

"I don't know, maybe?"

"Carter, Eliza isn't one of your barflies."

"I know that."

"Then why are you treating her like one?"

"Treating her like… How is asking her out a bad thing? I just tried to snag a date that way since she said she wasn't interested."

That sound. Carter *hated it* when Lincoln made that sound, sort of a cross between a sigh and a grunt and something else completely chock full of censure.

"When did Eliza say that?"

Ah, man. Would he ever learn to keep his mouth shut? "The, uh, night you and Mac went to pick up the girls and I tagged along."

"When you walked Eliza to her room."

"Yeah."

"You *tried* something with her that night?"

Carter's mind slid back in time to his first glimpse of Eliza in her tipsy state. She'd sat there with her dark hair and flashing green eyes. Beautiful, soft, classy—yet adorably kissable. "Not really."

"When the answer's not a simple no, it's a lie. You'd known her, what, five seconds?"

Carter wiped a hand over his face and rubbed. "I flirted with her. Okay? Come on, Linc, she's beautiful. If she'd given me the go-ahead that night, I would've hung around. What guy wouldn't?"

"Someone who cares more about the person he's with than just getting laid. That's who."

"It's not like that. Not with her."

"No?"

"No." But of course Lincoln would think that way. The guy had been married way longer than he'd been single.

"Carter, Eliza is best friends with Marsali, which involves Mac, which means this isn't a game."

"I never thought it was," he said, getting angry.

"You just said you would've taken her up on an offer even though you knew she'd been drinking *and* we were waiting downstairs for you to return."

"I *meant* I would've enjoyed hanging out and getting to know her."

"Getting to know her?" Lincoln repeated, sliding Carter a suspicious glance.

"That's what I said." And it was true. One look at Eliza told him she wasn't his usual "type," but he was drawn to her all the more because of it. "Look, maybe it's you and Amelia finding each other after all these years and getting married, but it's really got me thinking about things. You're right about the women I've been with in the past, the ones I attract hanging out where I do."

"And? What about them?"

Yeah, Lincoln was going to make him spell it out. "I don't want that," Carter said. "Not for me and definitely not for Piper. Eliza… When I saw Eliza, I *liked* her. Just like that."

"That's called lust."

"It was more than that," he countered. "We talked the whole way to her room. We talked on the beach. She's different. Fun. Smart. But she shuts me down at every turn."

Lincoln was silent a moment before he spoke.

"You mean she isn't falling for your tattoos and pretty face like all the others."

He shrugged. "The tats definitely don't seem to help with her."

Lincoln leaned his head back and laughed so hard it echoed off the back side of the house.

"I love it. Finally!"

"Finally? What's that supposed to mean?"

"It means you may be on to something. Eliza's making you work for it, brother. I like her even more now," Lincoln said, wiping his eyes. "Oh, that's good."

"Is it?" Because it didn't feel good to him. It felt

like rejection. And nobody liked rejection. The kid on the beach was right about that.

"Any woman who winds up with you needs to be able to give as good as she gets," Lincoln said. "And I understand your thinking. Logically, Eliza's already been vetted by Marsali since they've been friends so many years. Mac, too."

Carter agreed with a silent nod.

Lincoln stood up and swung his chair around to face Carter before sitting back down and digging his elbows into his knees.

"I'm playing shrink here, okay? Humor me and listen. Because Eliza *is* like every other woman."

And here he'd always thought Lincoln was the smart one. "Come again?"

"She sees the outside first, and one look at you tells her a lot. Like the fact you're one of those guys who's never had to work all that hard to score—which isn't her thing and more proof she's not like the women in your past."

"So what do I do?"

"If you want a quality woman, you have to bring quality to the table."

Carter stared at his brother, not liking the thoughts in his head. "I am who I am."

"You're not a bad guy, Carter. I'm not saying that. I've watched you mature a lot in the last ten years, especially the last five since Piper's come along. You've got a great head for business. You're a fantastic dad."

"Okay. So how do I get Eliza to see that?"

"You stop coming on to her, at least until Amelia and I are married."

"What?" Carter asked. How was he going to get closer to Eliza if he wasn't allowed to... *get close*?

"I mean it," his brother said, his voice a low growl of warning. "You are hands-off. Amelia is stressed enough trying to get everything done without having our wedding planner quit because Eliza is uncomfortable with you coming on to her too strong."

He didn't like it. Now that he'd set his sights on Eliza, he wanted to follow through. Pursue. Step up and go after the life he wanted for him and his baby girl. He felt like a racehorse being held in check when all he wanted to do was run. "What else?"

The question came out as a grumble.

"Once the wedding is over, don't charge at Eliza like a bull in a china shop."

Had Lincoln read his thoughts?

"You heard what Mac said about her ex. She's skittish and with good reason. So take it slow. One of the decisions Amelia made today was to accept Mac's offer of having the wedding here in his new backyard. Amelia and I are meeting with Eliza tomorrow evening. If you'll behave yourself, you're invited to come have dinner with us. Help Eliza out if you're around when she's here doing whatever she's going to do. Just do it with no expectation of getting something from her in return."

"I would've helped her with the arbor regardless," Carter said. He might have made some costly mistakes in his past, but he wasn't *that* guy.

"I know you would've. But by asking her out the way you did, you tainted the experience and you'll have to start over with her because of it. She's probably got her guard up now."

That she did. *Prickly* was a good way to describe her.

Carter wiped a hand over his face yet again. Why did women make things so difficult? Take offense so easily? "Fine. I'll do it. And you're welcome to use my yard, too. There's not much in it, so it has room for a tent or something if you need it."

Lincoln sat back in the chair. "Thanks. I'll let Amelia know. All she's talked about is that wedding she went to on Friday and how they had a tent and pillows and some kind of couch… I don't know. But she liked it."

"Whatever you need. Just tell me what else should I do with Eliza," Carter said, liking what he was hearing and wanting to get Lincoln back on track. At first he'd thought Lincoln meant for him to avoid Eliza altogether, but hanging out casually and letting her get to know him was a better idea.

"Keep Piper out of it."

The words brought out a frown. "Eliza knows I have a kid. Piper was with me on the beach. Besides, of all the women I've dated, Eliza's the only one I'd actually trust around Pip." He wouldn't have handed Piper off to Eliza to get ice cream had that not been so.

"I know. But if things don't work out between you and Eliza, Piper will be the one hurt the most. Keep her out of it. Let them be friends. Piper will see Eliza here in the future as part of the wedding and Marsali's friend, but keep her out of your personal life. Piper doesn't need to be put in the middle."

Carter got up and stalked to the edge of the tiered patio, staring off toward Lincoln's pool and the lights flickering beneath the water.

He needed to think, to plan and come up with a strategy of approach that wouldn't scare Eliza away or have her building her protective walls higher, one that would allow her to see him as a good guy.

One who doesn't cheat.

"What's rumbling around in that head of yours?" Lincoln asked from behind him.

Carter turned to face his brother and shook his head. "Just thinking maybe the cavemen knew what they were doing when they'd see a woman they wanted and claim her."

Lincoln chuckled at Carter's audible frustration.

It was true, though. Something inside of him had clicked the moment he'd first set eyes on Eliza. He wanted to know her secrets, what made her laugh. Protect her from the jerk who'd abused her trust and broken her heart.

"Just remember what I said. Going after Eliza means risking your friendship with Mac should things go badly. Make sure you're prepared for the fallout."

Carter shoved his hands into his pockets as he stared at his brother and slowly nodded. He understood the risks.

What he had to figure out was how he could convince Eliza to trust him and give him a chance.

Chapter 7

After a long and exhausting weekend of weddings that ended with a blessedly small but decently lucrative one on Sunday evening, Eliza walked to the kitchen table in Lincoln's house the following Monday a little before six and set down the many tote bags she carried.

Each held an assortment of wedding regalia, from invitation samples to table favors to popular color schemes and what could be done with them, her portfolio of photos including flower arrangements, food selections, and options. The list was endless.

Over the years, she'd accumulated quite a bit of leftover wedding supplies, given to her by brides who didn't know what to do with it all afterwards. Her three-bedroom home in Carolina Cove consisted of her bedroom and two storage rooms she could barely walk through.

Organizing her "stash" had been on her long list of to-dos forever, but she'd never found the time to make it happen. And though business had slowed due to her breakup with James, she'd filled the time with networking events in an attempt to salvage her career.

Eliza had just pulled the packs of invitations from the logo-ed material as the first item to go over with the happy couple when she looked up at the sound of a high-pitched squeal.

Piper played in the pool—with her gorgeous daddy. Her shirtless, tattooed, and impossibly muscular daddy.

"Like what you see?" Amelia asked softly.

Eliza flushed and ducked her head so that her hair hid her face, rummaging around in the bag to unload the rest of the samples. "Just checking o-on her. I heard her scream."

"Mmm," Amelia said. "I told Lincoln you were here. He's on a call but will be in as soon as he can. Oh, these are beautiful. It's going to be hard to choose," she said, flipping through the invitation sets.

"Since it's happening quickly, simple is best, but you definitely want to do something more than an e-vite."

"Yes. Absolutely."

"Did you give any more thought as to your color scheme?" Eliza asked, taking a quick peek out the window and struggling to not swallow her tongue.

Apparently playtime was over because father and daughter were now exiting the pool. Water sluiced down Carter's hard, muscled body, and his biceps bulged when he raked his fingers through his wet hair, the act delineating every taut muscle in his abs.

He had tattoos on both arms, though one of them snaked up his shoulder and onto his upper chest.

"But then maybe we could just have everyone come naked and bring in a Mariachi band."

"Mmm." Eliza blinked, her brain replaying Amelia's words and homing in on the last part of the sentence. "I'm sorry, what?"

Amelia grinned and shook her freshly high-lighted head at Eliza.

"He's a really nice guy. Just so you know," Amelia said.

Eliza forced her attention *away* from the window and shook off the awareness Carter's nearly naked body had brought about. "I'm not looking."

"Oh, yeah, you were."

"No, I mean… I suppose I *was* looking," she said, her face flaming hot, "but I'm not interested. In Carter o-or dating. That's not my focus right now."

"I see. Well, if you change your mind, just know that he's one of the good guys."

"I won't," Eliza said, settling on dumping the contents of the last bag she'd carted in. "Let's start with invitations, shall we? I brought ten of my favorites, but if those aren't to your liking, I have plenty more to look at."

"No, I like all of these. Especially… this one, I think," Amelia said, holding up a card featuring various pearlized seashells and starfishes, with gold seahorses, with silvery-gold script. "It's elegant, understated, and perfect for a coastal wedding."

"Awesome," Eliza said, lowering herself into a chair so she could open her wedding bible and begin Amelia's packet of information. Every detail went into the packet Eliza carried with her so that she was never without the bride's information and no mistakes would be made. "I have plenty of those on hand and can have them printed quickly. So did you have had a chance to pull addresses for your guest list?"

"I have, but, um, about that. Lincoln and I both have more friends and associates we'd like to include. Will that be a problem?"

More people meant more tables, more chairs, more flowers, more supplies, more invitations. "What are we talking?"

As though summoned by his fiancée speaking his name, Lincoln entered the kitchen from somewhere in the house.

"Eliza, good to see you again. Thanks for coming."

"Hi, Lincoln," Eliza greeted. "My pleasure. The

sooner we can make decisions on all of this, the better."

"Lincoln, do you have any idea on how many guests you're up to now?" Amelia asked. "Mine went up by twenty-two."

"Oh, probably the same number at least," Lincoln said.

At least? When the rule of thumb was always to round up, twenty-two equaled twenty-five. And twenty-five times two… "Fifty… on top of the forty we'd discussed?"

Carter and Piper entered the house, and Eliza found herself struggling to breathe once more. Didn't the man own a shirt? He had a towel wrapped around his neck, but it didn't cover nearly enough of him.

Add that to the guest list mushrooming at such a rapid rate, and she wondered if the tiny spots in front of her eyes were from stress or lack of food.

"Hey, you ready for a snack, sweetheart?" Lincoln asked his niece.

The little girl nodded before she spotted Eliza and came running over to her.

"Piper, you're wet," Carter said, his tone one of warning.

The girl gave her a damp hug, and Eliza welcomed the distraction since it gave her time to regroup from the change in numbers on a wedding that already pushed her physical limits. "It's fine,"

Eliza said. "Hugs are precious, damp or not." And she'd take all the hugs she could get right now if it would temper the anxiety rising inside of her like a tsunami.

She never wanted to disappoint a bride, especially not someone so integrated into her inner circle of friends the way Amelia was as Marsali's client and Mac's neighbor. But they hadn't even started planning and the guest list had doubled.

Eliza felt Carter's gaze on her, but she wasn't quite able to make eye contact.

"I went to school again today," Piper said.

"You did? How did it go?" she asked, focusing on Piper's sweet face.

"Great! But Mason fell down and hurt himself and he cried."

"Oh, well, I hope he's okay," Eliza said, unsure of what else to say.

"He is. He got a big Band-Aid, though. It had turtles on it."

"Piper, let's let Eliza work while we get that snack," Carter said. He placed a large hand on his daughter's shoulder and gently steered her toward the fridge.

Eliza tried not to focus on the fact that, as he did so, she was on eye-level with his abs.

"Well, one thing to mark off the list is the venue. We're having the wedding here," Amelia said. "Well, at Mac's. He's offered us the use of his yard."

"Carter, too," Lincoln said to Amelia. "Which made me think of how much you liked the tent at that wedding on Friday. There's plenty of room to do that there."

"Oh, there is!" Amelia said.

"Maybe we could have dancing around the pool here, the wedding in Mac's yard, and a tent with food in Carter's?"

Lincoln made it sound so easy, but he was talking about *three* different stations that would need setup, and... a tent? *That* tent? The fourteen-months-to-plan tent?

It wouldn't have been such a demanding thing to consider had she not lost yet *another* of her part-time employees to James's new business venture as her competitor. She'd have to find help, and—

"That would be perfect!" Amelia said. "I hadn't had a chance to tell Eliza about Mac's offer, but how great would that be? We won't have to scramble to find a venue, and I could get ready here in the house. We could store everything here or maybe Carter's as it arrived? I hate to impose but—"

"Fine by me," Carter said from his position across the room.

"Eliza? What do you think?" Amelia asked.

She thought it was fourteen months of planning squeezed into less than two weeks. The venue change was nice and worked in their favor, but securing tents for the date could be tricky depending on scheduling, not to mention catering since they weren't using a hotel…

"Wasn't that wedding huge?" Carter asked. He'd lifted Piper onto a stool, where the little girl now ate a banana. "Kind of over-the-top?"

"Yes," Amelia said, "but we wouldn't do anything nearly that elaborate."

Eliza inhaled and forced herself to gather her dwindling energy reserves. "I will do whatever you need me to do," she began, "*but* I need definitive numbers. And you'll have to choose a menu by the end of tonight so I can contact caterers, and once that's established, there's no changing things without serious cost increases." And stress.

"What if we didn't do a sit-down dinner," Lincoln said. "Make things more casual?"

"She still needs numbers," Carter said.

Eliza made eye contact finally and realized with a pinch in her heart that he was taking up for her. Trying to get the happy couple to realize the time crunch was definitely an issue. The problem? She didn't need his help. "Hors d'oeuvres would be easier," she said. "And give us a lot more breathing room to make any last-minute changes because we could supplement shortages from local restaurants."

"I like that," Lincoln said. "I always try to support local businesses."

She exhaled and managed another breath as the tightness in her chest eased. "Well, going that route, we could actually set up something with a few waiters roaming with edibles and champagne," she said, thinking on her feet.

She could probably hire waitstaff from the restaurants themselves, people looking for extra cash for a couple of hours' work. "That wouldn't require a full dinner menu, which would require renting plates and utensils and the like."

"I like the sound of that," Lincoln said. "So long as Amelia agrees."

"Yes," Amelia said immediately. "Especially the part about the ease of adjusting for changes. The more people find out, the more they express an interest, and I hate to be the one saying, 'No, you can't come.' Especially when one of them is Oliver Beck."

Marsali's Oliver? Interesting.

And great publicity. But his presence would mean less likelihood of no-shows because attendees got to rub shoulders with the A-list actor.

That kind of free publicity could definitely increase business.

And since paid publicity wasn't something she could afford right now, it made getting this wedding just right all the more important. "Okay, that would definitely be the best way to go. So we're thinking a tent for Carter's yard, standing tables intermixed with regular, and three hundred chairs to scatter between the three yards with emphasis in the ceremony and tent area?"

"Yes, that sounds perfect," Amelia said, her expression filled with bridal excitement. "What's next?"

Eliza inhaled and braced herself. "Menu. What are we eating at this reception?"

Chapter 8

Carter made himself at home in Lincoln's kitchen and set to work on fixing dinner. The steaks had been set out earlier, and by the time the food was ready, he figured Eliza would be due a break.

He wasn't sure how she did what she did, but as a contractor who'd spent more than his fair share of time going over house plans with clients who constantly changed their minds or saw some great new thing they wanted to add due to Pinterest—something that happened a lot with his job these days—he empathized with Eliza.

Amelia wasn't demanding in any way, but one glance at her expectant expression made it clear Eliza was having a hard time setting boundaries due to the time crunch. She wanted to keep her clients happy—always a good thing—but there had to be limits.

He noticed a break in the conversation and took

advantage of it. "Eliza, how do you like your steak?"

Her head jerked in his direction, and he watched her gaze drop to the platter piled high.

"Oh, you don't have to—"

"We planned to," Amelia said. "Dinner for all of us. Mac and Marsali are coming over later."

"Amelia, we have a *lot* to go over," Eliza said.

"And you will," Carter said. "But you have to eat."

"Yes," Amelia said. "So we will feed you while you ask us questions."

Eliza seemed to take a moment to come to terms with the dinner plans and finally shrugged.

"Okay, thank you. Um, medium to medium well," Eliza said.

He nodded and grabbed the platter to head out the door. Piper hopped down from her seat and followed him with her bottle of water. While he opened the door for Piper, he caught Eliza's gaze on him and felt a surge of pleasure. Maybe he was egotistical, but he could tell she liked what she saw, even if she pretended otherwise.

By the pool, he opened the grill he'd started before going inside and got to work, his thoughts on the plans being made. He'd never had a big to-do like the one Amelia and Lincoln were planning, and it made him wonder what Eliza's dream wedding would be like. Big and fancy? Small and intimate?

Doing what she did, it made sense that she'd

want something like no one else. She was unique, after all, and having planned so many weddings and made so many brides happy over the years, she'd no doubt given a lot of thought to her own and deserved to have something fancy for herself.

A bit later, Carter sent Piper in to tell the adults the steaks were about ready and rolled the corncobs one more time. He couldn't wait to see how Eliza ate hers. Delicate little nibbles? Cut it off and eat with a fork? Dig in and chomp down?

The door opened onto the screened-in patio, and everyone emerged carrying something. Plates, glasses, drinks, utensils.

Eliza carried one of her three-ring binder books, and when he joined them, he realized it had Lincoln's and Amelia's names on it. "Had to bring it with you, huh?"

"Every minute counts," she said.

They settled in around the teakwood table on the screened porch. Carter walked around the group, delivering their custom cooked meat.

"These look fabulous," Amelia said. "And the corn? Yum."

"Dig in," he said, using the fork to place Eliza's on the plate in front of her. "Medium with a shade of well."

"Thank you."

Once everyone was served, he loaded his own plate and took the spot opposite Eliza, noting she deftly cut her steak but didn't so much as look at the corn.

"I love fresh veggies," Amelia said. "Though you're not helping me keep things low-carb with this."

"You don't need to worry about that," Lincoln said.

"Agreed," Carter added. "Men don't want to cuddle stick figures."

Eliza avoided eye contact and kept chewing.

"Oh, Carter, while you were grilling, we decided on colors," Amelia said. "Mostly white and sand, with hints of gold and blue. I'm thinking a tulle gown for Piper. Blue to match her beautiful eyes."

"Will it have a poofy skirt?" Piper asked, butter running off her chin.

"You can have the poofiest skirt available," Amelia said.

"And be the most beautiful flower girl there ever was," he said to his daughter.

Carter felt the moment Eliza's gaze landed on him, but when he shifted his attention to her, she averted her gaze once more.

She still hadn't touched her corn. Surely she wasn't one of those women who didn't like to get a little messy? What about ribs? Seafood?

Sex?

"Izzy and I are going shopping tomorrow to look for a wedding dress," Amelia said, referring to her best friend. "You're welcome to join us, Eliza."

"Can I come?" Piper asked.

"You'll be in school, kiddo," Carter said. "But you'd better believe Amelia will pick out something pretty for you, too."

"Definitely," Amelia said.

The subject changed to what the groomsmen would wear and how Lincoln would differentiate himself from the pack. Carter listened with half an ear, not really caring what he wore.

His gaze locked on Eliza, and he watched as she eyed the corn like a project she was about to undertake. "Not your favorite?"

"Too messy."

Hmm. He happened to like some things messy. But what was more, he got the distinct impression by the way she was eyeing it that she would've chowed down on the corn had no one been around, so messiness had a place with her, but not where everyone could see.

Really? Comparing the way she eats—or doesn't eat—corn on the cob to other areas of life?

It made him wonder, though. Because that first night when he'd met her, she'd been *tipsy* and her guard had been down. Eliza had been *messy* and messy looked good on her.

Now she appeared much too professional, not to mention stressed, and he wouldn't mind seeing her with butter on her soft, kissable lips. Or hair wet and stuck to her skin in the pool.

When dinner was over, the half ear of perfectly

grilled corn remained on Eliza's plate, and he mourned not getting to see her eat it.

"Oh, I'm stuffed," Amelia said. "Eliza, can I get you anything?"

"No, I'm fine. That was delicious. Thank you."

The thank-you was said to him, and Carter dipped his head in a nod.

Everyone gathered plates and glasses, and he and Eliza were the last at the table.

"Next time I'll cut the corn off the cob for you."

She lifted her head at his words, and her eyes widened a bit before she shook her head. "That's… thoughtful but not necessary. I just didn't want to seem unprofessional when I'm on the job."

"What about when you're not working?"

A smile tugged at her lips. "Grilled corn is a huge favorite, actually."

A laugh left his chest. "So basically you sat there being tortured through dinner because you didn't want to be messy?"

"Yup."

He paused at the entrance to the house, her comment drawing his attention to her lips just like it had that night in the elevator. Was that only a few days ago? Given how many times she'd wound up in his thoughts, it seemed like a lot longer.

"Um… I should probably get in there so I won't be here all night."

"You can always sleep over at my place." The moment the words came out of his mouth, he wanted to take them back, but it was too late. And he hadn't meant them like _that_. Well, he wouldn't be opposed to that but still… "On the couch. Or spare bedroom. Not… Sorry."

A low laugh emerged from her, and she shook her head as she slipped by him into the house.

He watched her every move, taking in the sway of her hips as she walked back to the kitchen table.

Across the room, Lincoln cleared his throat, and Carter looked up to find his older brother shooting him a dark glare. Carter sighed.

The next two weeks were going to be a whole different type of torture.

Chapter 9

Over the next couple of days, Eliza found her thoughts drifting to a certain tattooed and gorgeous man.

The planning session with Amelia had lasted a good hour and a half after Carter had excused himself to take Piper home to get her bathed and ready for school the following morning, but even after he'd left Lincoln's home, Eliza wasn't able to completely relax.

During the evening, she'd found herself noticing the similarities between Carter and his older brother. And given how many there were, seeing Lincoln so sweetly interact with Amelia left Eliza wondering if Carter would be the same way. Could be the same way?

His blunder in inviting her to stay had brought more than one smile to her lips in the time since because he'd seemed so sincerely awkward afterward. And awkward on Carter wasn't something she'd consider a normal occurrence for a man who looked like he did.

The brothers intrigued her as a whole. Lincoln was just as handsome as his younger sibling, but he didn't have the edge Carter carried. One born of... difficulty?

Eliza learned through Amelia that Lincoln's first wife had passed away, so he'd had a hard life, too. Especially considering he'd raised his twins alone the last three years.

But why the rougher edge with Carter? What had honed him to such a degree?

Curiosity killed the cat. And considering she'd told Carter she wasn't interested, she couldn't exactly ask, because that expressed interest. Maybe she could get some info on the down low from Marsali?

You know what'll happen if you so much as mention his name.

A knock sounded on her door and she glanced at the clock. Lincoln was right on time. Some of the items Amelia had chosen from Eliza's portfolio were pieces Eliza had created or purchased and now kept stored in her spare rooms as rentals.

Eliza was thankful Amelia had chosen them, too, since it boosted her income from the event. Lincoln had volunteered to stop by and help her load the boxes into his truck and her van for transport to his house. With less than a week and a half left, every moment counted. Thankfully once the small weddings booked for this weekend were over, she could focus fully on Amelia and Lincoln's.

Eliza glanced in the mirror by the door and smoothed her hair before swinging her front door wide. "Lin—uh, Carter?"

"Hello, Eliza," Carter said in his deep, gravelly voice.

His gaze swept over her quickly before shifting back to her face, taking in the sundress she'd worn for the day's errands. "What are you doing here? How do you know where I live?"

The corners of his firm lips tilted up, and he gave her a patient-looking grin.

"I saw your van."

"And you just knocked on the door? What if this was a client's house?"

"Lincoln mentioned he was picking up some boxes from you at this time, and I had a job to check on down the street. After seeing your van, I put two and two together and offered to do it since I'm already here."

"Oh." Well, that did make more sense than where her mind had gone but—

"Can I come in?"

She inhaled and stepped back. "Of course. I'm sorry, I was just surprised. I, um, got most of the items out earlier, but there are a couple of things you'll have to help me get. They're quite heavy." Normally she would've had James or Clarissa or

Kellie help her with such things, but since James had taken off with her trustworthy crew…

"Not a problem."

Carter stood there and stared at her, and with a start, she realized he waited on her to lead the way. She did a mental eye roll at her nervousness and headed toward the bedrooms.

It wasn't like she hadn't had a man in her home before. But something about Carter's broad shoulders and those eye-popping tattoos on his bulging arms left her pulse racing and insides quivering.

Finally they made it to the storage rooms and she turned to find his gaze low—on her behind? She watched the way his gaze quickly shifted upwards and locked on hers, seemingly unapologetic.

Men. They were all the same, weren't they?

She twisted the knob and stepped back to allow him to enter without her. "Those four boxes right in front. The white box on the left, and in the other room are the heavy boxes containing glassware and some other props. The settee will have to be transported, too."

"You've got quite the stash," Carter murmured, eyeing the room.

"Things added up over the years, and since I wasn't using these rooms… I do wish I had shelving to better organize it, but that's on a mile-long list of to-dos, especially now that I'm… restructuring my business," she said, trying to stay politically correct and not sound bitter. "I'll, um, have to do more digging later to get the rest of the items."

She watched as Carter bent and lifted the first bulky box in his arms, then scrambled to get out of the way, back down the hall, and hold the door open for his exit. She noted his red logo-ed truck parked behind her van and watched as he loaded the first box into the back.

On his return, Carter removed his cell phone and moved his finger over the screen.

"Your shelving issue... I'm working a job and this is part of the stuff they're getting rid of. It's free, and it might work for what you need," he said, handing her his phone.

His long finger swiped through a couple of images as she watched. "Free?"

"Yeah. Want me to load it up and bring it to you? I can put it in your garage until the wedding is over and then help you get it inside and ready for your boxes and bins."

Ah, but what did he expect in return? "Uh, that would be great but I'm not sure I can hire you right now."

"Eliza..."

Did he have to say her name that way?

"The stuff is free. And you taking it will help me to get it out of the guys' way."

"But your labor costs—"

"Plan a party for me."

She blinked at him. What? "Excuse me?"

"Look, I'm not worried about it, but you apparently are so… I know you don't do birthday parties, but how about in exchange for labor and whatever storage you need me to come up with, you plan Piper's birthday party? She wants everything mermaid, which goes along with a lot of the beach stuff I saw in there."

She blinked at him, unsure of what to say. "I…"

"Look, she's turning five, and it would be a great way for her to get to know some of her classmates and for me to meet their parents."

Eliza stared down at the shelving that would be perfect for her needs before she handed the phone back. She crossed her arms over her chest, waited for his gaze to shift downward, but surprisingly, it didn't. "You do realize a birthday party for a five-year-old is way easier than what you're going to have to do to set up storage for all of my stuff."

"Easy for you," he countered. "Do I look like I know how to create a mermaid party? That stuff," he said, lifting the phone and the images she'd just perused, "is easy for me. Come on, even exchange. How about it?"

Well, it *was* better than him asking her on another date. "Nothing else?"

A wry smile flashed over his handsome face and shot her pulse into orbit.

"Nothing else. And for the record, I'm sorry if I made you uncomfortable. I shouldn't have asked for a date last Saturday after the arbor *or* invited you to stay over."

"You flirt. A lot."

"Only with certain people. And never with bad intentions," he countered, holding her gaze. "But I am sorry if I've made you uncomfortable."

She really wasn't sure what to make of the apology, only that he seemed sincere.

"Okay, next box," he said when she remained quiet. "You think about it and let me know if you want to make a trade. I'd have one happy girl on my hands if you could work some magic and bring her mermaid party up a few notches from just cake and ice cream."

The last was said with wry bemusement, and she realized the older Piper got, the more into girlie things she became—and the more out of his depth Carter probably felt. The majority of single fathers would have no clue how to do the cutesy, feminine stuff girls loved. But for Piper? "I'll have to check my schedule but... I accept your offer."

Carter grinned and a look of supreme relief flashed over his face.

"You're a lifesaver."

"Yeah, well, you may regret the swap when it comes to making storage that works for me."

"It'll be worth it to see Piper's face."

She held the door for him to enter and get the next box, and his long strides carried him down the hallway. Carter might be too handsome for his own good, but no one could deny his love for his daughter. And like it or not, she admired that about him.

"Eliza?"

She blinked up at him, only then realizing she'd stood there and ogled his masculine form every step of his return. "What?"

His gaze narrowed on her, sparkling with something she couldn't quite name along with quite a bit of amusement.

"You gonna open that door?"

Chapter 10

Carter transported the boxes of wedding stuff to his truck, including the boxes she'd claimed required two people to carry, and entered Eliza's one last time to schedule delivery of the shelving to her. He watched as she checked her phone and then her paper calendar, and realized that, despite losing half her business to her ex, Eliza still had networking and bridal events to attend along with meetings for future weddings, cake tastings, and whatever else a bride and groom might want or have on their agenda.

The calendar pages were filled with neatly scribbled notes, and as he stared over her shoulder, he might have noted the location and times of two back-to-back bookings this coming weekend at a local hotel.

The guys needed to take Lincoln out for a low-key bachelor party anyway, so why not at the same location where Eliza would be?

A plan formed and he nodded to himself. Eliza was off-limits at least until Lincoln and Amelia were married, but nothing said he couldn't make use of the time by getting her to see he wasn't a bad guy. And handy to have around in case she hadn't been able to replace the hired help she'd lost to her ex?

"Okay, so, you said her birthday is September first. You're in luck. I actually do have that Friday open," she said, tapping a finger on a page where something had been erased.

"You sure?" he asked, hoping to get more info.

"Yeah." She rolled her eyes and pasted on a smile that didn't brighten her eyes. "Another event lost to the ex. My loss is your gain, though."

She bent and wrote Piper's name on her calendar. In ink. And he couldn't help but be impressed. A wedding would be a lot more lucrative than a kid's birthday party done as a favor. "What happens if you get another last-minute wedding like Amelia and Linc's?"

Eliza straightened and met his gaze, tilting her head to one side.

"I won't cancel on you. When I take a job, I'm there."

He dipped his head in respect and tried not to want more from her. At least not at the moment.

As though he wasn't the only one noticing just

how close they stood to one another, Eliza wet her lips and took a step to the side.

"Um, okay, so is this a surprise? Or do I need to consult with Piper on her wishes?"

He thought about it a moment before shaking his head. Eliza had enough demanding brides in her life without adding a precocious five-year-old who wanted to be a real-life mermaid. "Let's keep your involvement a surprise. I've got a pretty good idea based on things she's said. I'll write it down and bring it when I drop off the shelving."

"Okay. Does she have favorite colors?"

"She's got this sequined mermaid tail she wears to play dress up." He pulled out his phone again and scrolled through his pictures until he found the right one. "There. She loves that thing."

"Ah, jewel tones are my favorite," she said with a smile. "And I do have plenty of tulle and supplies already. This will be a nice break from the norm. I'm glad you asked."

"I'm glad you accepted the trade-off."

Silence followed his words and continued long enough to become awkward. "Okay, so, I'm going to get this stuff to Linc's. If you need me to take anything else, just let me know. I'll be by again, checking on the job as it progresses, and Mac and I will both pitch in wherever we're needed. It's not a problem."

"Thank you."

He stepped back and noted the mix of industrial-style metals and beachy-looking woods mixed in her house. He'd always liked building things, and her style of decorating was a favorite of his. Nothing too feminine but functional and pretty all the same.

"I'll, uh, see you out."

He took one last glance at her calendar for a quick refresher and then followed her toward the door. "See you soon, Eliza."

"Yes. Drive safe."

Carter finished loading and started the engine to head home.

"Took you long enough," Lincoln said when Carter arrived and opened the door minutes later.

"Seriously? Have you been out here waiting for me this whole time?"

"Just tell me you didn't do or say anything you shouldn't have."

"I didn't," he said with a gentle slam of the truck door. "I actually apologized for anything I said that made her feel uncomfortable and... it went well," Carter said, moving to the back of the truck. "Eliza and I even came to an agreement."

"An agreement? So you *did* come on to her?" Lincoln asked, glaring at Carter.

Carter lowered the tailgate and loosed the straps securing the boxes. "No. I had to go in and dig some of this stuff out. She's got wedding stuff stored in two spare bedrooms and mentioned needing shelving—which I happen to need to get rid of off a jobsite."

"So what's the agreement?"

Lincoln's tone revealed his hesitation in asking.

"Eliza wouldn't agree to just take it, all right? I tried, especially since it's free and in my way. So, we swapped labor and shelving for her amping up Piper's birthday party."

Lincoln groaned.

"Hey, it was the only thing I could think of, and making Piper's party bigger and inviting the kids from her class will give me a chance to meet the parents of the hoodlums Piper's going to school with. I want eyeballs on these people for when she gets invited to stuff."

Carter loosened the last strap and turned to find his brother staring, his hands on his hips. "What?"

"Nothing." Lincoln leaned into the truck bed to grab the first box. "I was just thinking you might have handled that perfectly."

"Yeah?"

"Yeah."

"Then now's a good time to tell you we're having a bachelor party for you Saturday," he said, naming the hotel where Eliza's bookings were taking place.

"Why there?"

Carter shrugged. "Just thought it would be a nice place."

Lincoln's gaze narrowed shrewdly.

"This wouldn't *also* happen to have something to do with Eliza, would it?"

Busted. "It… might."

"Carter—"

"She mentioned losing her help to her ex last weekend, and when I picked up the stuff for you and Amelia, I noticed Eliza had a couple of weddings booked this weekend."

"At that hotel?"

Carter reluctantly nodded.

"So having my bachelor party there means us being around if she runs into a snag?"

Once again, he nodded and gave Lincoln a sheepish shrug.

His brother chuckled and hefted the box he carried higher against his chest. "I have to give you credit, little brother. When it comes to women, you do have a romantic side. That's why it's always gotten you into trouble."

Chapter 11

The week flew by way too fast for Eliza. Before her breakup with James, they would do setup together, both of them in headsets, organizing the crews of caterers, chair and table deliveries, florists, and the like with precision coordination. Six months later, she was still trying to find her own rhythm and keep eyes on everything at once, especially since her last full-time employee, Kellie, had left two months earlier—another sneaky underhanded hire by James.

She had schematics, detailed times of when each group was supposed to arrive, and timers and reminders set accordingly, as well as plans for holding areas while setting up.

But like most scheduled things, someone was inevitably late due to traffic or loading or employee issues. And then there was the fact Eliza had yet to find a replacement for either her assistant or assembly/setup help. Three people she'd used in the past had answered her calls but weren't able to help, and two others had simply not responded.

Ah, the joys of owning her own business.

"Eliza? These guys need to know where to go," one of the florist's assistants said as she walked by.

Eliza turned and spotted the very large instruments. *Crap*. Just when she'd thought she had a handle on things. How could she have *forgotten* about the cello players?

Her gaze shifted to the chairs being set up, all of which would have to be shifted because the bride had specifically asked for them to be placed just to the right of where the ceremony would take place. "Stay cool and hydrated inside for now," she said with a smile. "Then up front exactly forty minutes before the ceremony so you're seated and playing at thirty."

Both men nodded and hefted their instrument cases to return to the interior of the hotel while Eliza bolted for the sand. She needed to catch the chair delivery guys before they— "No, no, *no*," she said, searching for them and not seeing any of the black-shirted employees.

Really? *Really?* They hadn't even hung around to check out the girls by the pool?

She stashed her binder on the first seat of the first row and got to work. Thankfully there were only fifty chairs. She could do this.

Two rows in, she heard someone calling her

name and looked up to find Carter, Lincoln, and Mac heading her way. What on earth? "What are you doing here? Are you guests?"

The trio grinned. Well, two of the three. Mac looked a little disgruntled.

"Nah. We came for Linc's bachelor party but saw you rearranging things. Need a hand?" Carter asked.

Eliza blinked at them, and before she could agree or disagree, the three men went to work shifting the white chairs several feet away from their present position, matching her placement pattern.

"Haven't been able to hire new help, huh?" Carter asked softly as he worked beside her.

"I interviewed someone but they didn't work out. Par for the course these days."

"Well, we'll be here all day and tonight if you need us to pitch in on something else," Carter said.

She paused so she could meet his gaze. "What about Piper?"

"She's with Amelia tonight. They're having a sleepover."

Eliza didn't have time for the relief that flooded her system. She prided herself on doing a good job and providing the beautiful weddings she promised her clients, but when everything seemed to be working against her, she knew better than to turn down help, even if she'd rather not need it.

"Eliza, what about these?" Mac asked.

She turned and found Mac and Lincoln

standing on the other side of the aisle. "Same distance that way," she said, pointing. "Have to showcase the cellists because they're friends of the bride."

With four people shifting chairs, the process didn't take long. "I can't thank you enough," she said to the men now standing there looking at her, each of them wearing a sheen of sweat due to the end-of-August heat.

"It's no problem," Carter said softly. "We each own our businesses, and we know what it's like when you're short manpower."

"Well, it's appreciated, gentlemen. I'll be sure to send a round of drinks on me tonight. For now, I have to get back to work."

"Text me if you need anything else and we'll come back out," Carter said.

Eliza happened to be looking Mac's way and noted how her best friend's older brother glanced at Carter before sliding his gaze back onto her.

Eliza took the look to be one of protectiveness, but considering her state of disinterest in men presently, the effort was wasted.

"Yeah, we'll be around," Mac added dryly.

Lincoln and Mac murmured their goodbyes and began heading toward the hotel. Eliza walked to the front to retrieve her binder. She held it to her chest and turned only to run into Carter. "Oh!"

His hands fastened on to her elbows.

"Easy there."

"I thought you'd gone. With them," she said with a tilt of her head.

"Have you eaten today?"

What was it with him and food? "I had breakfast."

"It's five o'clock, Eliza."

Already? Guests would start arriving any minute.

She shook her head and took a step back. "And I have too many things to do. I'll eat later." Her gaze landed on the florist, who'd arrived forty-five minutes late. "I *have* to go, Carter. Thanks for the help. Again."

She slipped by him and hurried to meet the woman carrying half of a pre-made floral arch.

This wedding was much smaller than the ones last weekend, but the bride had gone a little crazy with her flower requests.

Once the arch was in place, white columns were carried across the sand and still more flowers placed atop them as well as along the two ends of the arches. Creamy nautical rope was strung along both sides of the aisle and attached to the sides of the chairs, then decorated with eucalyptus sprays, ribbons, and seashells.

The clock ticked as things fell together with frantic intensity. Guests began arriving but lingered back toward the shade provided by the hotel. Once the sun sank lower, more of the seating was shaded and guests began to move forward.

Eliza checked her charts and lists and finally felt comfortable enough to leave the beach to venture inside to the bridal suite. She liked to check on her Bs and Gs beforehand, just to get a feel for the mood of the day.

As she passed through the lobby, Eliza glanced toward the bar area and saw Mac, Carter, and Lincoln sitting at a high-top. As though sensing her presence, Carter's gaze locked with hers and her stomach did an odd flip.

Lah, the man really needed to come with a hazard warning.

She managed a smile and kept moving, her mind on the thoughtfulness of the trio of bachelors who'd come to her rescue. One in particular.

Maybe it was the way he'd helped out his brother or offered to trade shelving for a birthday party for his baby girl, but she was beginning to observe a different side of the gorgeous contractor.

But, that being said, Carter had seemingly taken her warning and backed off, and she was grateful for that.

Wasn't she?

Chapter 12

Carter kicked back in a chair in the hotel lobby around ten that evening and watched the sliding doors leading out to the sand open and close for the millionth time with no signs of Eliza's return.

She'd gone a hundred miles an hour the entire night, first with the wedding outside and then with the reception inside. Dance music pulsed from the other side of the closed ballroom doors, and Carter spotted the two musicians from the wedding hitting on bridesmaids across the room. By all measures, Eliza had pulled off a beautiful and successful event. Again.

"This has got to be the worst bachelor party ever," Mac said, sending Carter a glare.

"It's fine," Lincoln said, staring at his cards so hard Carter wondered if he was trying to memorize them. "I didn't need a party anyway."

"Will you stop looking for Eliza?" Mac demanded. "It's annoying."

Carter locked gazes with the other man and realized Mac knew exactly why they were there. "Did you take a look at her? A real look? She hasn't eaten all day, she's exhausted, and she has another wedding here tomorrow."

"And just how do you know that?" Mac asked, gaze narrowing.

"Gentlemen, can we stop bickering and play cards?" Lincoln asked.

"No," Mac stated. "I thought I warned you off of Eliza?"

"You can't warn me off of her," Carter said. "She isn't your toy."

"She isn't yours, either."

"Trying to win here," Lincoln muttered.

"Yeah, well, you'd better watch it. The last thing she needs is you messing with her when she's still getting over the last guy."

"Best way to get over someone is to—"

"Seriously? You're going to go there?" Mac said, glaring at Carter. "She's practically—"

"Your sister?" Carter asked, hammering home Eliza's brotherly kiss comment.

Mac glared at him. Carter glared back. "Look, I have no intention of hurting Eliza. Besides, I can't make a move until after Linc's wedding, so chill."

"It's true," Lincoln murmured. "I axed his plans until Amelia and I are on our honeymoon."

"Which means once Linc and Amelia are gone, you're going to do what?" Mac asked.

"Dude, you had your chance. Actually, as Marsali's big brother, you've had lots of chances with Eliza over the years, and it didn't work." Mac all but growled at him and Carter shrugged. "Just stating facts."

"Yeah, well, fact is if you hurt her, I will hurt you. Got it?"

"*Or* you could let Eliza take care of herself and stay out of her business," Eliza said, her tone cold as ice.

Carter stilled and turned to face Eliza, her expression filled with feminine ire.

"Really? Are you three seriously sitting here discussing me like… *that*?"

Carter glanced around and noted all of them had sat back in their seats and now stared at Eliza as though eyeing a tiger suddenly loosed in the lobby.

Carter cleared his throat, brain scrambling to soothe. "We meant no offense, sweetheart."

"I'm only looking out for you," Mac said.

"I was told there was a bachelor party," Lincoln grumbled under his breath.

Eliza's arms were loaded with an elaborately wrapped wedding present and Carter stood. "Let me carry that for you."

"I've got it," she bit out, fingers white.

"Eliza—"

"I have work to do. Please leave me *out* of future conversations—and plans."

He followed her as she walked away from them. "Hey. Hey, wait a second. Eliza, I just want to be your friend."

A huff left her, and the look she shot him blew his statement to bits.

"Friend?"

"Fine. I admit I'd like more—to get to know you."

"*Why?*"

He blinked at her question. Drew back from the intensity behind it. Why? "Because you're you and I like what I see."

"Yeah, well, you're you and... I don't. Bad boys are just... *bad.*"

Eliza turned on her heel and stalked away as quietly as she'd approached.

"Ohhh, yeah," Mac said, chuckling hard. "Okay, I think I've seen what I needed to see, *brother.*"

Lincoln tossed his cards onto the table. "I'm going to go call my fiancée."

"I'm going to the bar to drink to Carter's epic shutdown," Mac said, standing.

Carter swiped his drink from the table, glared at Mac's back, and decided he had a wedding reception to crash. His conversation with Eliza wasn't finished.

The inside of the hotel ballroom was lit by

massive amounts of carefully placed lanterns, string lights, and table candles. As he took it all in, he wondered how Eliza had managed to pull it off without working herself into the ground the last several days straight.

He scanned the carefully lit interior and found Eliza by the gift table. She looked perfectly put together in a strapless knee-length dress, her long hair pulled up with tendrils framing her face, and sparkling earrings that swung as she turned her head and spotted him approaching her.

He moved toward her, holding her gaze the entire time.

"What are you doing?" she asked the moment he stood close enough to hear her. "This is a private event."

"I thought you could use some help as things wind down."

"Carter—"

"Have you slept at all the last couple of days?"

Her mouth firmed before she took a breath, and no amount of money or willpower could keep his gaze off the act in that dress.

"Not much," she admitted. "But you need to leave."

"How did you get all of this put up?"

"I hired a couple of the hotel's maintenance guys to set up after hours. Thankfully the room wasn't booked beforehand so they allowed me to get in last night."

"Well, I'll help you take it down and you don't have to pay me."

She blinked at him and shook her head. "Carter, why are you doing this?"

"Maybe I'm trying to prove to you I'm not as *bad*," he said, quoting her, "as you think I am."

She winced. "I'm sorry I said that. It was rude."

"It was honest. But you're wrong about me, Eliza."

"Am I?"

He inhaled. "I have a history. Everyone does. But who I was isn't who I am now. Why won't you let me help you?"

"I don't… want to *owe* you."

"You won't. You shouldn't feel that way. Ever. Like I told you outside on the beach, I have a business I started from scratch, and I know what it's like when help doesn't show or gets lured away by the competition. Or," he added, lowering his voice, "costs more than you might be able to afford while trying to regroup."

She crossed her arms over her front. "So you're only here asking to help because you feel sorry for me?"

"I suppose that's… part of it."

"And the rest?"

He chuckled softly. "Maybe I'm a little interested in getting to know you better."

"Oh, yeah? I heard your discussion with Mac outside."

"Mac and I talk smack all the time."

"Yeah, well, smack talk or not, men don't typically help women without ulterior motives."

"My only motive is to get to know you. Look, you've obviously been burned. So have I," he said, taking a step closer and getting a whiff of her perfume. "But right now, I'm just trying to prove to you I'm a nice guy so that when you're ready, you'll give me a chance."

One of the couples carried their dance off the plank floor and bumped into Eliza, shoving her into him.

Eliza's hands unlocked from her front and braced against his chest as she caught herself. Carter tucked her closer still and stared down at her, a fire sweeping through him at the feel of her pressed against him.

Her gaze lowered to his mouth and her lips parted. He watched it all, wondering if she felt the same chemistry firing his blood. "Eliza?"

"*Eliza?*"

Her name echoed as the male of the couple who'd bumped her turned toward them.

Carter glanced at the guy but felt Eliza's nails dig sharply into his shirt and skin as she stiffened up like a board. She held on to him, hesitating a moment, before she simply turned her head. Carter watched as Eliza struggled to maintain her composure when she faced the man—couple—now standing a few feet away.

"James…"

James? Ex-boyfriend/business partner/cheater James? Carter wrapped his arm around Eliza's shoulders and cuddled her close while he held the man's gaze and kissed the top of her head. "Sweetheart, aren't you going to introduce me?"

Chapter 13

Of all times. Of all people…

Eliza inhaled and struggled to come to terms with the fact James and Clarissa stood within inches of her, side by side and looking far too smarmy, in her humble opinion.

She'd considered herself lucky to have avoided them for so long, but tonight her luck had obviously run out. "Of course. Carter," she said, finally finding her voice, "this is…" *my lying, cheating, can't-be-trusted ex and his ho…* "James and Clarissa. They're former business associates." Taking the high road sometimes sucked, and this was definitely one of those times.

"Carter Hayes," he said without removing his arms from around her to extend a hand in greeting. Carter held her pressed to his side, and while she wasn't sure how he'd known who the couple was other than by reading her reaction to seeing them, she welcomed the support, both physical and emotional.

Seeing one's ex was never easy, especially with their fling at their side. But having Carter at hers was definitely better than facing them alone.

"Hayes Construction?"

"That's the one."

"Beautiful reception," Clarissa said in her baby-ish voice.

"Thank you," Eliza said, squeezing the words out between semi-gritted teeth. "Why are you here? I don't remember you being on the list."

"Oh, you know. Checking things out. I have a client wanting something like this, so I took some photos."

"Of *my* event?"

"Just for visuals and possibilities. Look, no hard feelings about my luring the setup team over to our new venture, right?" James asked, shooting Eliza his seemingly charming wolf's grin. "I mean, they work hard and deserve to get a little more than they were earning so…."

"That they do," Eliza said, a smile pinned to her face because she would not give James the satisfaction of seeing the pain he'd caused her. Not only personally but financially.

Betrayal was betrayal, and the man was scum, but what was worse was that she had to accept the fact she had been taken in by his charm and flattery and put up with his narcissistic abuse for far too long.

But now? He wasn't her problem. And had Clarissa not willingly and knowingly cheated with someone involved with someone else, Eliza would've felt sorry for her and what was to come when James treated Clarissa the same way.

"Nah, man, you did her a favor. No worries about that," Carter said. "You have more than enough help now. Right, sweetheart?"

Eliza glanced up at Carter and found his gaze locked on James, the two men seemingly battling it out silently. Like it or not, she compared the two, with Carter clearly the better-looking winner.

Clarissa apparently agreed, seeing as how she couldn't take her eyes off of him. Eliza noted the young woman's perusal of Carter's broad chest and brawny arms revealed by the steel-gray short-sleeved polo he wore. The color complimented his eyes and dark tan.

"Well, that's good to hear," James said.

Eliza watched the other woman's expression take on a flirtatious, catch-me-later look Carter would have to be dead to misunderstand, and a hot flash of anger tore through Eliza. There was a name for women who acted like that.

"Sweetheart?"

Carter lightly squeezed her, pulling her from her

dazed state. When his statement finally sank in, Eliza lifted her face and met his gaze, uncaring that Carter was laying it on a bit thick. "Mmm, I do," she said. "Carter and I work *very* well together."

The statement was one of truth, but the throaty drop in her tone as she stared up at Carter with adoring eyes was purely show. At least that's what she told herself. Because fact was… once again, the man had come through for her.

From building the arbor last weekend and doing a quick change with the chairs earlier to making it look as though she wasn't alone and running on fumes, Carter had shown up for her. Proved himself with actions rather than just empty promises.

And right now? She just wanted James to suck it.

Carter's expression revealed his awareness of her flirtatious tactic and he was amused by it. He tugged her close and kissed her head again.

"If you'll excuse us," Carter said to the couple. "This is our song."

Song? Now they had a song?

Oh, and it was one of her favorites, too.

Carter guided her toward the dance floor, and she was very aware of his hand sliding to her waist as he drew her to him while Ed Sheeran's crooning voice filled the ballroom.

"I'm the wedding planner. I shouldn't be danc-ing," she murmured just loud enough for him to hear.

"We're in a dark corner," he whispered, his lips brushing her ear. "Besides, it's the last song. The bride and groom left while we were talking to your ex, so most everyone is packing up to go themselves. Don't you want to rub a little salt since ol' James is over there glaring at us?"

He was?

It took massive amounts of willpower not to immediately turn back to look. Instead she smiled up at Carter as he pulled her flush against his long, lean, *gorgeous* body.

"Don't look now but I believe they're having a lover's spat."

A peek in James's direction told her Carter's words were true, and she felt a slight thrill of satisfaction given the pain and devastation they'd pummeled her with. "Thank you. For… that."

"I meant every word."

She stared at him, uncomprehending.

"You'll have all the help you need. I'll see to it. Plus, since my guys and I are licensed in all sorts of things, you can think bigger, expand the realm of possibilities for your couples. You name it, we'll price it and figure out how to make it happen."

Wait, what? She lost herself in the glinting depths of his dark gaze. "What are you suggesting?"

"I have a couple trustworthy young guys on my crew either working their way through school or working side hustles to pay off debt. Between me pitching in and you hiring them whenever you need extra manpower, we should have you covered as far as your setup and breakdown needs. As to design specialty, we can play it by job. No partnerships," he stressed. "Just an added benefit to being my friend."

"Friends with… benefits?"

He gave her one of his bad-boy grins and she literally felt her knees go weak. "I… don't know what to say."

"Just think about it. Linc says I have a brain for business, and it seems to me if you're looking for a way to get an edge over your competitors, my offer might give you one. Am I right?"

She nodded, knowing it was true without having to do much pondering.

"So, maybe it's time to scale up and show everyone what you're capable of. Especially old James over there."

Carter was right. He was sooo right! Her mind spun with possibilities. With that kind of guaranteed design help, she could do… *any*thing! Electrical, structural, fountains? And anyone with the cash to expect those types of things meant a whole other pricing tier.

She sucked in a sharp breath of excitement, and her senses whirled with the scent of his cologne. Sandalwood teased her nose.

The subtle scent made her think of woods and water and nature. That special moment when time and space and everything disappeared and she was able to just *breathe*. No worries. No fear of what the future might bring.

Here. Now. In this defining moment... she knew, one way or another, she was going to be okay. Because she wasn't alone, and her prayers had been answered in the form of her too handsome rescuer.

Tears stung her eyes and she blinked them away, let herself be drawn even closer to Carter, her head tucked under his chin. His strength surrounded her. His breath warmed her ear and sent shivers down her spine as they swayed back and forth in time to the music in the best slow dance she'd ever experienced.

But was it because she was with Carter? Or because of the sheer relief she felt at having a plan?

The song came to an end, and she blinked when the band did a loud riff and said their good-nights. She stopped and took a step back, shocked at how easy it had been to lose herself the last several minutes. How easy it was to forget her fatigue and exhaustion from burning the candle at both ends and running on fumes because her pulse now pumped with possibility. "I should... I have stuff I have to do."

"I'll help."

"Carter... aren't you supposed to be hosting a bachelor party?"

He smiled at her and her entire body warmed in response.

"Linc is fully aware of why we're here. I'm sure he and Mac will be in as soon as they see everyone leaving."

She blinked at him. Simply astounded. He'd done that, brought his brother and Mac *here* on the ruse of a bachelor party, because of her. To help *her*. Whereas James had come to take photos of her event no doubt so he could pass them off as his own.

A laugh caught her by surprise. She didn't know if Carter's statement was stalkerishly weird or adorably sweet. Her heart really wanted to err on the side of sweet, but her mind still screamed at her to be wary. "How did you know I'd be here today?"

She watched as Carter grimaced and then shrugged.

"I may have looked at your calendar the other day when you scheduled Piper's party."

Stalkerish it was. But still sweet. "I see."

"You know why, Eliza."

Because he wanted her. But want and desire were fleeting. And as a man who was obviously used to getting his way with women...

She inhaled again and glanced around but saw no signs of James and Clarissa. "You do realize that even if I accept your offer to up my wedding planner game and we work together, I learned my lesson with James. We'd have to keep things strictly professional."

Carter's jaw clenched at the news. "Okay," he said, frowning. "Deal's off."

She shook her head at him, smiling because she just couldn't help herself.

"Or maybe with time, you'll realize I'd never do anything to deliberately hurt you," he added.

The air left her lungs because of the intensity of his gaze, and she tilted her head to one side, forcing herself to shake off her gratitude for earlier, the coziness of the dance, and see him as the whole dangerously bad-to-her-senses package. "So you say. But what'll happen when you finally accept that I'm not going to just fall into bed with you?"

"I accepted that the first time I met you," he countered. "It's one of the things I like about you, Eliza."

She faltered and gaped up at him, surprised by his matter-of-fact statement.

Was it true, though?

The dimples came out when Carter smiled at her, and she braced herself for impact.

"Sweetheart, any man in his right mind would want more from you. But all I'm asking for is a chance," he said. "Time for you to get to know me and see me for who I am, not just what you think you see."

Not just what she… She sucked in a sharp breath and realized she had been pretty focused on Carter's bad-boy looks. Maybe there was more to the man than his handsome face?

Her mind flashed back to that moment before James had said her name. That moment when Carter had been about to kiss her and she had been about to let him.

"Eliza?"

"I have work to do."

Chapter 14

Eliza's wariness and distrust plagued Carter into the next day when he watched her do her thing with the skill of an orchestra maestro.

Last night, Mac and Lincoln had arrived as Eliza had skittered away claiming wedding-planner duties, but between him and the guys, they managed to get Eliza to bed by one.

Alone. Which, having walked her to her room on the third floor, was saying something.

She'd been so adorably rumpled and exhausted all he'd wanted to do was climb into bed and hold her until he had all of the answers he wanted about how she'd wound up that way. His gut told him it was more than just what had happened with her ex, and Carter hated that she'd experienced that ugly side of life.

He'd gone up to the suite he'd booked for Lincoln and took the pullout since Mac and Linc were both already snoozing in the queen beds. Just punishment for involving them in the first place, no doubt.

This morning, he'd called a couple of his guys, Mac had contacted Marsali, and Eliza had looked appropriately shocked when the group appeared to help set up for wedding number two. Lincoln had offered to stay, but Carter had sent him home to his fiancée since they had their own wedding to prepare for and things to be done.

Once Eliza's shock had worn off, though, Carter could've sworn he'd spotted a sheen of tears she quickly blinked away.

Exhaustion would do that, though. And he hoped she didn't burn out before getting her business back on its feet.

While the hotel staff handled table arrangement and covers, Marsali tracked the florist, Mac and Carter's guys set up an indoor gazebo, and he and Eliza unboxed the lanterns, battery-operated candles, hardback books painted the same color for uniformity, and greenery that would be the table arrangements since the bride was a librarian and the groom an avid reader.

He'd thought the books strange as decor at first, but when Eliza explained, he realized it was a sweet statement for the couple's interests.

"Okay, last one," she said, opening the Post-it-numbered box.

He had to give Eliza credit. For all the chaos

involved with the setup, everything was organized and flowed well because of the effort she'd put in beforehand, as well as the timing so that the florist and catering crews weren't tripping over each other.

Tables completed, he stepped back and took a look at the way the room was being transformed so quickly. Beautiful yet very different from the one last night. "You're amazing, you know that?"

Eliza blinked up at him, a smile forming on her beautiful lips. "That's what all the boys say."

He watched her turn on her heel and carry the now empty box toward the others to be stored behind the scenes, every step a saucy sway of her hips that brought salacious thoughts to mind. "I'll bet they do."

FOUR HOURS LATER, breakdown began. It didn't take nearly as long as the setup, and Eliza was grateful, because every part of her body ached at this point. If not for Carter and the rest of the team he'd assembled, it would've been impossible to get everything done on time. Eliza struggled to breathe when she realized how close she'd come to royally screwing up a wedding. "Are you sure I can't hire you?" Eliza asked Marsali. "You've got a serious knack for this."

"Can't. Sorry," Marsali said, folding a box top into place and holding it while Mac taped it up.

"I'm happy to pitch in when I can, but you know I'd much rather get them here than anything."

It was true. Marsali had a God-given talent for matching couples, and it would be a shame for that to go to waste because she was doing other things. "Can't blame me for trying. Every time I hire someone, they drift away, thanks to James."

"Can they drift back?"

Eliza lifted her head and turned at the voice belonging to one of her former employees. "Oh. Uh, hey, Kellie. What are you doing here?"

The young woman looked decidedly uncomfortable, as well she should considering she'd left Eliza in such a lurch by not giving notice.

"I saw some tweets about the wedding and… Eliza, I owe you a huge apology. I'm *so* sorry. I never should've left, especially the way I did, but James insisted and… he promised a sign-on bonus and better pay but…"

When the woman's words trailed to a stop, Eliza raised her eyebrows and waited. "But?"

"Well, I'm still waiting on the sign-on bonus, and as of this week, they're two paychecks behind and all we hear are promises. Things aren't… They're not going well there."

Well, isn't that interesting? "How is that possible with all of the weddings he took from the business?"

"You haven't been reading his reviews, have you?" the younger woman asked.

And have them rubbed in her face? "No, I-I didn't want to read them after all that happened." Eliza was vaguely aware of Carter, Marsali, and the others listening to their conversation, but since Kellie wasn't worried about privacy, why should she?

"I get it. But you should know James and Clarissa are hit-and-miss at best, and people are starting to get ticked off because of it. Some of the events were handled so badly the couples are demanding refunds, and others are beginning to cancel because of all the screwups and the rumors going around."

The statements should've made Eliza feel better. Maybe they did somewhere deep inside, but the fact that it came at such a high cost left her far from pleased when it all could've been avoided. "Rumors?"

"That they're using the money for personal use and not paying the vendors, or substituting cheap items for the more expensive ones they're paid for. That kind of thing. Look, Eliza, I'm sorry. I know I screwed up and I'll have to earn your trust again, but I'd really appreciate a second chance. I've learned my lesson and I *really* want to come back. I'll do whatever you need me to do."

Eliza hesitated but only because of fear. Kellie was a good employee—minus the whole quitting-without-notice thing. She'd always come early, left late. Done above and beyond what was asked of her. "How do I know you won't walk out and do the same thing again?"

"I guess you don't." The twenty-something inhaled and glanced at the others listening before shifting her feet and turning to go. "I understand. I just wanted to apologize in person because I owed you that. I'm sorry to bother you."

"Kellie, wait." Eliza watched as the girl turned, a hopeful expression on her plain yet pretty face. "You're hired—but on probation. *One* screwup and—"

"Totally. I understand! I'll even sign something stating I'll never leave without giving notice. Whatever you want, I'll do it."

"Are you free now?" Eliza asked.

"Yes, ma'am," Kellie said, smiling.

Eliza tilted her head toward the boxes and bins and all of the other stuff slowly being piled near the door. "You know the drill."

Eliza watched as the girl ran toward her to give Eliza a quick hug before she got to work.

Eliza turned to find Carter watching her, a small smile pulling at his lips. "What?"

"Nothing."

"That look means something," she murmured.

A sexy, rumbling laugh emerged from him as he leaned toward her and lowered his voice. "You gave her a chance. That bodes well in my favor."

"Kellie isn't a threat to my—" She broke off and inhaled sharply, wishing she'd kept her mouth shut and just walked away. Instead she'd just revealed way more than she ever wanted to. "I mean—"

"I know exactly what you mean, sweetheart. But you thinking I'm a threat means you're not as *un*interested as you let on."

"I'm not. *Carter*," she said, trying to finish the conversation without drawing attention.

But Carter turned and walked away whistling, and Eliza raised and lowered her hands in a gesture of frustration.

"He so has the hots for you," Marsali said.

Eliza closed her eyes and counted to three. "Not interested," she said, turning to face her friend.

"Oh, yeah, right. The man deserves a medal. You do realize the strings he's pulled for you this weekend? Favors from friends? Calling up his own employees?"

She had. Who *did* that?

"And all while he's under oath," Marsali said.

Eliza stilled. "What does that mean?"

"Carter promised Lincoln he'd leave you alone until after the wedding because Lincoln didn't want you running scared if Carter came on too strong."

"*That's* leaving me alone?" she asked, waving a discreet hand in Carter's direction.

"For a man like Carter?" Marsali smiled. "Yes. That's why I can't wait to see what happens next week after the wedding is over."

The thought left Eliza struggling to breathe. She had a hard enough time focusing whenever she was around Carter, even though his behavior was apparently his "tame" approach. "You're twisted to be so sweet, you know that?"

Marsali's laughter rocked the nearly empty room.

"And *you* are a softie behind all of those walls. I wonder if Carter has figured that out yet?"

Chapter 15

Carter had figured that out. In the days following, Carter often found himself pondering Marsali's comment about Eliza and thinking of Eliza's tender heart beneath the protective walls she'd built.

He'd seen her compassion and caring multiple times during their time together because it was such an integral part of her. It came out when she spoke to her girlfriends, to Piper, to anyone she *didn't* feel threatened by. But anytime he got close, the walls went up along with her wariness, and he'd learned to recognize the look as it happened.

Chaos ensued as Lincoln and Amelia's wedding approached, and Carter used every opportunity he could to get closer to Eliza.

Because fact was, he couldn't stop thinking about how close he'd come to kissing her before her ex had so rudely interrupted. Technically, kissing her would've broken the promise he'd made to

Lincoln, so Carter was glad it hadn't happened. But the clock was ticking, and soon his restraints would be lifted. While his brother counted down to the wedding, Carter counted down to getting another opportunity to kiss Eliza.

Soft, feminine laughter filled his house, and he smiled at the sound. Amelia, Kellie, Marsali, and Eliza were in the back of the house doing wedding stuff and having a blast.

"Daddy?" Piper asked, her pink-tipped fingers pulling her mermaid doll close as she shifted to one side on the bed.

"What, baby?"

"My dress for the wedding is *really* pretty, isn't it?"

He grinned at her and bent to kiss her forehead. "Your dress is pretty but nowhere near as beautiful as you are."

"I'm smart, too, right?"

"You better believe it. Why are you asking?"

"Do you think when I get big someone will want to marry me?"

"I'm sure they will. But hopefully not for a long, *loooong* time," he said. "Did you say your prayers?" He knew she had because he'd listened to them like he did every night. He dreaded the day when she broke the ritual. Because as a man who'd made a lot of mistakes, he now knew the value of that quiet time.

"Yup. I asked God for a husband like you 'nd Uncle Linc."

"Whoa. *Husband?* Too soon, baby girl. I'm not ready to let you go yet. How about you stick around for twenty years or so?"

"That long?"

He chuckled at her complaint and drowsy-eyed gaze. "Yeah, that long. You need to grow up and do some things before you go off and get married."

"What things?"

"Oh, I don't know. Maybe get your first big job after school or go on a trip you want to take. Things that help you figure out who you are and what you want."

She yawned and turned her freckled nose into the mermaid's hair.

"I don't want to go to bed," she said, eyes mostly closed and fighting every blink. "Is Eliza going to be here tomorrow night, too?"

A noise alerted him to someone in the hallway, and he glanced over his shoulder, spotting the beautiful brunette standing outside Piper's door, watching them with her soft green gaze. "I think so since we're all helping to get ready for the wedding."

"Good. I like her."

Carter smiled, his gaze on Eliza. "I like her, too."

He saw the way Eliza's lips parted at his comment before she ducked her head and disappeared from view. Carter refocused on his daughter and tucked the sheet around her shoulders, letting his hand drift over her bright hair as he leaned low and kissed her forehead. "Sweet dreams, baby."

Piper made a soft, sleepy sound, her lips pursed as she finally let go and settled into slumber. He stood carefully to not jostle the twin bed and left her room, pulling the door shut behind him.

Back in the living room, Carter watched as Amelia and Eliza fussed over the small bouquet Amelia's best friend, Izzy, would carry as maid of honor.

So many little details, each of them part of a bigger whole.

"Oh, wow. Look at the time. I have to go, too," Amelia said. "Filming starts soon and I *have* to be there since I won't be the rest of the week or next."

"It's fine," Eliza told her. "No problem."

"I hate to leave you when Marsali and Kellie just left, but I have to make sure we're good to go for when I'm honeymooning."

"This is what I do, remember? Go do what you do," Eliza said.

Amelia quickly hugged Eliza before heading out the door. Carter watched as Amelia sent him a grin over her shoulder before shutting the door behind her.

"Time for a break," he said to Eliza. "You've been going nonstop since you got here. How about something to drink? Water? Wine? I may have some sodas."

"Water would be nice," she said. "Thanks."

He moved to the fridge to retrieve a bottle for both of them, but as he crossed the room, he noted the way she wouldn't quite look him in the eyes.

"Um… you know, I have a lot of work to do before I call it a day. Maybe I should take it to Mac's since—"

"No." Carter slid a hand over his hair and tried to make his loud blurt sound more relaxed than it was. "I mean, all the stuff is here, so it just has to be carried straight out the door the day of, right? There's no sense in moving it only to move it again."

Eliza bit her lower lip and worried it between her teeth. Something he wouldn't mind doing to her himself.

"I just don't want to wake Piper… or intrude."

It was early yet, but Piper had school and his daughter was a sleepyhead, which made an early bedtime essential to getting her moving in the morning. "You aren't intruding. And you definitely won't wake her. Once she's out, she's out. Been that way since day one. Getting her settled down is the hardest part. She goes until she literally crashes."

Eliza grabbed a box and opened it before getting another.

"What's all this?" he asked, indicating an oversized bottle he spotted in one of the boxes.

"Instead of a guestbook, guests leave a message for Lincoln and Amelia. The bottle is sealed at the end of the night, and they open it on their first anniversary and read the notes."

"And those?" He lifted his head in a nod toward her new project.

"Gourmet chocolate wedding favors. They need bagged, tagged, and then added to the baskets."

"Would you like some help?"

Eliza's gaze flicked toward his then away again.

"Uh… sure."

He washed his hands and then donned a pair of plastic gloves. "I'll bag, you tag? I doubt I can make them as pretty as you."

"Okay. Sure. Two chocolates in each."

He set to work, and it wasn't long before he figured out the quickest way to stuff the seashell-shaped chocolates into the tiny bags since it wasn't as easy as one might think.

Carter finished another bag and moved to set it between them right when Eliza reached for another, and their hands brushed.

"Sorry," she said, withdrawing.

"No problem. Eliza?"

"What?"

"Tell me something about you." He waited and when she finally met his gaze, he willed her to maintain contact this time.

"Like what?"

"I don't know. How'd you get into this?"

The question seemed to be less personal than she was expecting and she visibly relaxed a bit.

"Oh. Well, I started out working for a hotel as a teenager. I was a front desk person, but one day the event manager needed help, and I jumped at the chance to get out from behind the counter. The pay sucked, but I loved it. Within a week, I was the new event assistant."

"That's great."

"It was," she said, "until I kept getting blamed for the coordinator's screwups. By then I was a senior in college, and I decided if I was going to take the hits, I wanted to actually *be* responsible for them, so I started my own company."

"Your own company? You were what? Twenty-two as a senior?"

A small smile tilted her full lips up at the corners, and he found himself struggling to focus.

"Yeah. It was hard. I roomed with four other girls at the time, and space for stuff like this was at a minimum."

"And James? When did he come along?"

She rolled her eyes and yanked the strings of the bag.

"James and I met when I went to a hotel to scout it out for a couple. He worked in hotel management. We dated casually for about a year and..."

Carter waited. And then waited some more. "And?"

"I didn't trust my instincts. I was about to break it off with him when he asked me to be exclusive. I said yes, because it bothered me that we weren't, and convinced myself we were on track to becoming more. I found out later, the hotel he'd worked for sold to another and James had lost his job. In the meantime, I'd agreed to let him come in as a partner, to help me, because… well, because I thought we were going to be the power couple of event planning, I guess. So stupid."

Carter let her words hang in the air for a long moment, giving himself time to process them. She really did have reason to be wary of entanglements. "I'm sorry that happened to you."

"Me, too." She tied the strings of another bag.

"You know you're not the only person to ever do something stupid, right? Especially when it comes to relationships."

"I know. But with my past… I should've seen the red flags. I *did* see them, but I ignored them and told myself I was making mountains out of mole-hills. But I wasn't. And I have to own the fact I messed up so badly."

"Owning it is one thing, letting it keep you from living out the rest of your life another."

Her fingers stilled and he watched as her lashes lifted.

"Is that experience talking? I didn't mean to eavesdrop on you and Piper, but I heard you after I left the bathroom and…"

"Are you asking about Piper's mom?"

"Yeah. I mean, if you want to tell me."

He liked that Eliza wanted to know more about him and asked him personally, rather than Marsali. Or maybe Marsali had already told Eliza the story, but either way, he liked that she asked. "We met. Went on two dates. She got pregnant and we got married. Then Piper was born, and a week after we'd brought her home from the hospital, Piper's mom announced she didn't want to be a mom after all, and she split."

Eliza's sharp inhalation revealed the shock expressed by her beautiful gaze. So apparently Marsali hadn't filled her in.

"She just... *left her*? You? Does she see Piper? Come visit?"

"No. She signed over her parental rights with the divorce, and we haven't seen her since."

Eliza's lips parted and he saw the empathy and pain she couldn't hide.

"I can't imagine. I can't even..."

He nodded, because he couldn't imagine walking away, either. The pregnancy had been an accident, but from the moment he'd known he was going to be a father, everything had changed. It was like someone had grabbed him up and shaken some sense into him, and he'd tried to become a better man every day since. He'd thrown himself into being a good husband, a good provider. But it hadn't been enough. "I don't know what I would've done without Lincoln and Jill that first year. Piper was colicky. Man, that kid has some *lungs*," he said with a wry shake of his head. "But she's been the best thing to ever happen to me."

Eliza inhaled and tilted her head to one side as she met his gaze, a small smirk brightening her features.

"You probably get quite a bit of attention being a single dad of an absolute doll. Don't tell me that doesn't go a long way in scoring you dates."

He laughed, feeling more than a little sheepish. "It's had its moments."

"That you took full advantage of, I'm sure."

"I'm no saint," he admitted. "But from the day I knew she existed, my life changed. I committed myself to marriage and Piper, and I'll commit myself again when the right woman comes along."

"That's… admirable."

Something about the way she said it… "You don't believe me?"

"No, I… I have no reason not to."

"But?" If she had something to say, she needed to say it.

She plucked at the strings with her finger, staring down at the bag she held.

"But people tend to mean what they say at the time—until it's not convenient for them anymore."

His heart pinched at the expression she wore. "James isn't the only man who broke your trust, is he?"

An uncomfortable-sounding laugh emerged from her, and she grabbed another bag.

"Can anyone ever truly be trusted?"

"So you plan to live out your entire life afraid to love?"

"I'm not—"

"Who's lying now?" he asked, his gaze direct, holding hers, willing her not to look away.

"You've been there," she acknowledged with a lift of her chin, "so you know what it's like. Why would you or I or anyone risk that level of hurt again?"

"Come on, really? What about Lincoln and Amelia? You can't be one of those people who think you have one chance and that's it."

"I'm not but… I warned you I was cynical. You know, let's change the subject. Please."

He sat back in the chair and studied her, wondering how to crack the protective shell walled around her. "Not yet. How many guys have you dated since you and the ex ended?"

Carter waited, watching her. Eliza didn't speak. And then it dawned on him. "No one? Seriously?"

"How many women have you dated since— Wait, I seriously *don't* want to know the answer to that."

"Hey, it's not as many as you obviously think," he said, not liking it that she thought of him that way. "I'm a single parent and self-employed business owner. That doesn't leave a whole lot of time.

What's your excuse? Why haven't you gone out with anyone? I know you've been asked."

"I… have."

"But you turned the poor guys down and broke their hearts because you're afraid?"

"I've been working nonstop to salvage what was left of my business."

"Okay. I'll give you that. But you don't have that to worry about now. You've rehired Kellie," he said, referring to the woman who'd appeared at the hotel last weekend and worked from his living room tonight, "and I heard you tell Amelia that some of the people who'd originally gone with James are now rescheduling. So, once the wedding is over, we're going out."

"Who says?"

"I do."

"And if I disagree? What, are you just going to throw me over your shoulder like a caveman if you show up and I refuse to go?"

Reminded of what he'd told Lincoln that night a week or so ago, Carter bit back a grin. "Only if I have to. Come on. We'll be two battle-weary new friends who are just hanging out."

"A business dinner? To discuss my ideas and what might be involved in the design?"

"Sure. We'll even split the check if you like."

"You'd actually be okay with that? No funny business?"

Funny business? Oh, he could be all about the

funny business with her. "Hey, I'm not the one who hasn't dated in a while," he said, winking at her. "How do I know you'll be able to keep your hands to yourself?"

"You're incorrigible."

"So what's your answer?"

"I'll go... to discuss *business*."

Carter grinned. "Okay. Sounds like we have a date."

Chapter 16

"You're going out with *Carter*?"

Marsali practically screamed the question the following evening. Eliza glared at the cell phone on the tiny stool beside the soaking tub and rolled her eyes. *Well, that news certainly didn't take long to travel.*

"Eliza? Hello?"

She moaned and slid deeper into the water. "We're going out for a *business* dinner because I have designs I want to discuss with him. How'd you find out?" she asked, her tone revealing her upset with herself for allowing a pair of slate-gray eyes and a wicked smile to sway her.

But combined with the fact Carter Hayes had opened up to her with his story about Piper's mother—well, dinner shouldn't be such a big deal. Misery loved company, right?

She sipped her glass of wine and tried not to think about how Carter would look dressed in his best-man clothes in a few days' time. Or the fact she couldn't wait to see him wearing the hand-crafted leather suspenders Amelia had special ordered.

"I stopped by Mac's on my way home. Carter was there."

"And my name came up how?" Eliza pressed her damp hand to her face and rubbed hard. She'd rather Carter had kept his mouth shut but obviously he hadn't.

"Carter was telling Mac about how he'd run into James today."

Eliza sat up in the tub so fast water surged to the edge like a tidal wave. "What? Where? When? What did Carter say?"

Marsali laughed at the barrage of questions.

"On a jobsite, this afternoon, and he said he set James straight."

"About what? What does that mean?"

"You'll have to ask Carter."

"Marsali, tell me."

"I didn't get *all* the details. The story was mostly over by the time I got there. I'm sure Carter handled it fine. He's a good guy. You've got to see that by now."

"I know you know more than you're saying. Since when do you keep secrets from me?"

"Fiiine. Apparently James tried to work up a deal with Carter similar to one the two of you have —which, by the way, when did *that* happen?"

"It... Recently. Very recently. Things have been so crazy I just forgot to mention it."

"You think?"

"We haven't actually worked together or anything," Eliza said, explaining Carter's offer. "I've got some great ideas."

"That sounds awesome. And it definitely raises the bar for you. How exciting," Marsali said.

"Yeah. But James tried to *hire* Carter?" Seriously? Was the man ever going to hit rock bottom in his underhanded dealings? Just when she thought James couldn't sink any lower, he did!

"Yeah. And no worries, Carter said no. And a bit more would be my guess."

Eliza bit her lower lip and folded her arms on the side of the tub to rest her chin on top. "What makes you say that?"

Marsali's low chuckle warned Eliza that whatever her friend was about to say? She probably wasn't going to like it.

"Lizzie, you can lie to yourself all you want, but we both know you and Carter have some serious chemistry. When you two are in the same room, you can *feel* it."

"Chemistry isn't everything."

"No, but it's definitely important. Just... let yourself trust that you've learned from the past, and you'll make the right decisions in the future."

But would she? Because she'd made an awful lot of bad ones, and who was to say there weren't *more* in her future? "I… don't trust myself anymore. Not when it comes to men. I can't help it, I second-guess everything now."

"I get it. But Carter has been honest with you, right?"

"I suppose. How would I know?"

"Have you seen any red flags?"

"Other than the fact he's too pretty for his own good?"

"You can't hold that against him when he had nothing to do with it."

Maybe not. But she didn't have to *like* it. "It… scares me."

"You do realize you're beautiful, right? And besides, looks have nothing to do with cheating. Cheaters lack some very important things. Integrity and honesty. A grounded moral compass."

"I know that."

"Good. Because actions speak louder than words, and Carter has gone above and *beyond* for you, and not just with the weddings."

She closed her eyes and nodded to herself. He had. And even though it was sweet and friendly and *honorable*, a part of her still waited for him to change and not for the better.

"And if that's not enough, he's gorgeous and ornery and fun, and I think he's just what you need in your life."

"I don't *need* him." She'd made the mistake of

letting James convince her she needed him and look what happened.

"Eliza—"

"No, I'm cancelling. If we do the business stuff, we'll keep it professional. Meet in his office or something." *Not over candlelight.*

"Absolutely not. What will it hurt to go to dinner? He's someone I'd totally set you up with to get you out of your shell, as a practice date."

"Why do you hate me?" Eliza groaned, sliding back into the tub with yet another splash.

"Hate you? Seriously?" Marsali asked.

"Yes, seriously. I don't have a 'shell,' and my schedule is insane and not about to let up anytime soon. I don't have *time* to date, and yet somehow I agreed to a dinner, which means I'm obviously *not* in my right mind."

"Silly goose, your schedule is what you let it be and completely in your control."

"Says the woman who has me planning a wedding—which has grown exponentially, by the way—in two weeks for one of her clients."

"Well, there are a few exceptions to the rule, *but* that's a perfect example of why you should be dating, whether it's Carter or not. You can't work nonstop and never have any fun. Just don't lie to me and pretend you aren't drawn to Carter. I see how you look at him."

Drawn? Yes, but not in any way healthy to her well-being. Or future.

Or heart?

Eliza's mind filled with an image of Carter Hayes with his dark good looks, sexy smile, and inked biceps, and she groaned.

Did she admit to being attracted to Carter?

Yes.

Did it scare her?

Unbelievably so.

Because it wasn't just attraction she felt. It was the way he'd helped her, but more importantly, the way he treasured his baby girl and his brother, and how he'd stepped up for the mother of his child only to be rejected…

He'd *been* there. In her shoes.

And up until that point, she'd had the willpower to walk away from him from fear alone, but knowing he'd experienced the same kind of betrayal and walked through the fire and understood her fear because he'd lived it?

It was like something inside of her had just latched on and bonded instantly to the shared pain.

"You're becoming a boring workaholic who is so jaded you don't honor the love you work so hard to showcase with all of those beautiful weddings you pull together. You're filling your loneliness with busy-ness, and I'm seeing major signs of burnout. You see them, too, right?"

"Maybe." The word was a breath, soft and shallow.

"So," Marsali said, her tone changing over to

one of persuasiveness, "go have some fun and flirt —even if it's only as friends or business associates. Recover some of the magic behind *why* you do what you do. Remember how much fun it was in the beginning? The love and *romance*?"

"You think I'm just going through the motions."

"Aren't you?"

Eliza pinched the bridge of her nose and willed the nagging chronic headache to go away. Dang it, she hated when Marsali was right.

"Look, what James did was awful but he wasn't your equal to begin with."

"I know that. I see that now."

"Good. Because this thing with Carter? This is an opportunity to find something better. Even if it's just a *friendship* that shows you there are still trustworthy people in this world."

Eliza remained quiet, listening, pondering. Mulling over the wisdom Eliza had just imparted.

"Lizzie, do you trust me?" Marsali asked softly.

No, Marsali wasn't going to go *there*, was she? "You know I do, but—"

"No buts. Yes or no? And remember *years* of friendship weigh in the balance."

Tears stung her eyes, and Eliza blinked them away and blamed her upcoming period and stress and a diet lacking in chocolate—which she would rectify immediately. If she ever remembered to buy groceries. "You know I do."

"Then do this. For me. Because I want this for you."

She pressed both hands to her face, over her eyes, coming to terms with some hard truths. "I know you're right. Okay? I said it. Rationally, I know all men aren't sleazeballs, but—"

"It's *dinner*. With someone I know and trust and feel good about for you. Even Mac likes Carter."

"I'm not so sure about that."

"He does. He's protective of you, that's all. Because we know how hurt you were. The thing is, you will never heal locked down the way you are. You have to get back out there and *accept* invitations from gorgeous single men, even though the meticulous control freak in you can't plan or predict the future because it's not *in* your control. That's all part of the fun. Remember fun?"

Fun? Not really. And that was sad, wasn't it? "We need a change of subject," she said. "Tell me about you. Any more news on your book?"

Marsali was silent a moment before Eliza heard her friend exhale.

"My editor said they're getting lots of orders. Like, a *lot*. It's a little terrifying."

"That's great! And not terrifying at all."

"Okay, fine. Intimidating? Maybe that's a better word. I'm working on an outline for another idea now."

"I'm happy for you, Marse. Congratulations.

We'll have to go out and celebrate the day it releases."

"I'd love that."

"Mark your calendar. It's a date." The moment the words left Eliza's mouth, she winced because she knew it would bring Marsali full circle.

"Don't cancel, Lizzie. That's an order. Or a personal request. A plea? Whatever holds the most weight."

Eliza leaned her head against the back of the tub and stared at the ceiling.

Once Lincoln and Amelia's wedding was over, Carter would be freed of his promise to keep his interest in check. Which meant, when the time came, would Carter want their business dinner to be more?

Chapter 17

The days before Lincoln and Amelia's wedding day stretched Eliza's last nerve. She was on edge due to her impending dinner with Carter, her over-whelming desire for this wedding to be *perfect* because of her newfound friendship with Amelia, and the awareness that her business was finally righting itself with every new phone call that landed in her voicemail.

If anything, the break from James and his poor handling of all the clients he'd schmoozed and stolen had done her more favor. Because the clients who'd made that jump and regretted it now touted her skills and professionalism far and wide on social media, especially after she agreed to take them on again.

But with all of that whirling around in her mind, she'd come to a decision regarding her dinner date with Carter. And despite her thoughts on cancelling, she wasn't going to. Not only that, she was going to let the evening flow in whichever direction it might, be it strictly professional or… not.

Marsali was right. It was time to make a move forward into her future, and even though Carter had warning labels all over him, she couldn't help but think an evening spent flirting over candlelight with a gorgeous man would be fun.

But that was *after* the wedding. Before the wedding came… details and stress and rain, a steady downpour that had covered the Wilmington area and made it impossible to set anything up ahead of time to get a jump on the process.

Eliza, Kellie, and the crew had staged everything they could inside Carter and Lincoln's homes, even arranging the items so that everything would be carried out in the order it was to be set up.

Now Eliza adjusted her headset after the ceremony and watched the happy couple share a tantalizing kiss on the dance floor while staring into each other's eyes like no one else existed.

Marsali had said Amelia and Lincoln had a great story, and having learned it over the last two weeks, Eliza had to agree. They'd loved, lost each other for a time, and found one another again having learned countless lessons.

And if anyone deserved the perfect day for a perfect wedding, it was them. Maybe that's why it had been.

In her experience, every wedding had something go wrong. A broken zipper, a cranky ring bearer, or drunk groomsmen, *something*. But not this one. The rain clouds had moved on but left behind cooler temps, and setup had gone down without a single glitch. Like dominoes, the wedding preparations had taken place, each performed with military precision that left Eliza staring in rapt wonder.

"Catering is gathering up," Kellie said via the headset.

Eliza glanced at her watch, amazed to see that the night was almost over. Perfect weddings were hard to come by, and she was sad to see this one end. "Right on time. Thanks, Kel."

"I never knew headsets could be sexy," a deep voice murmured behind her. "By the way, I considered snagging one of those from your crew earlier just so I could talk to you."

Eliza turned to find Carter watching her, and she narrowed her gaze and lifted her chin. "Shouldn't you be flirting with the maid of honor? Or the photographer, perhaps?"

His devilishly handsome lips lifted in a smirk, and she bit back a telling sigh. The man looked ever so gorgeous with his dark tan, white button-down shirt, crisp gray slacks, and suspenders.

Amelia had opted for a beachy-boho-chic style that jived perfectly with her personality and profession as a set designer, which was why Lincoln's best man had wound up looking like a male model. The female photographer had loved getting shots of the brothers and taken quite a few of Carter by himself and with Piper.

Now that the ceremony was over and the reception wrapping up, Carter had rid himself of the bow tie, unbuttoned the shirt, and rolled the sleeves up his impressive forearms. And the picture as a whole?

Lawsy.

"Jealous?"

"Oh, no."

"Good. Because the only woman I want to flirt with is right here." He lifted a hand and indicated the beautiful setting. "I didn't see how you could top what I'd already seen you do. Thank you, for making their day special."

She couldn't stop the smile that formed at the praise and reveled in the success of the day. "It *was* gorgeous, wasn't it?" The day had definitely been blessed given all the things that could've gone wrong.

"Unbelievably so. Which is why..." He looked around, jogged over to a nearby bar area and swiped an entire bottle of champagne and two glasses from a tray, and returned. "We're going to celebrate. You are coming with me."

"Now?"

A low chuckle rumbled out of his chest, and he moved closer to where she stood. His cologne teased her senses even more and dragged her into the spell he cast.

Why couldn't she date him again?

"Yes, now. You haven't taken a break all day. And I want you to see something," he said.

"What?"

"Ah, Eliza. Trust me, it won't disappoint. Everyone knows their jobs, the guests are leaving as well as the bride and groom," he said, a lift of his chin indicating the couple waving goodbye to their guests as they headed toward Lincoln's home, freeing the well-wishers to stay or go as they pleased. "You can spare a few minutes."

It was true. Her crew—now back on track with Kellie as her second-in-command and Carter's two employees working as extras—would have no problem performing the remaining tasks.

"Come on. You know you want to."

He lowered his head, giving her a compelling look that made her ache to see how far he'd go to convince her.

"It has been a great day."

"Exactly. I heard about the magazine article."

Oh. Yeah, that news? The best. She smiled again and bit her lower lip, more than a little pleased with being featured along with Amelia and Lincoln due to their connections in film and local real estate. "That *was* a nice bonus for today."

"So what are you waiting for?"

Maybe it was the seemingly effortless day or the fact that things were finally looking up, or maybe it was the utterly breathtaking way Carter looked at her, but Eliza pressed a finger to her mic and told the gang she would be around but was taking a break.

The moment she removed the earpiece and set it safely inside of her bridal binder, Carter's calloused hand slid into hers. He tugged her away from the lights and into the dark toward the waterway. "Where are we going?"

She saw his smile flash over his shoulder and hurried along in her sensible flats as they crossed the back of the lawn to the wooden planks leading toward a dock. A boat bobbed gently up and down in the water. "Carter, I can't actually leave."

"We're not going anywhere," he said.

Carter stepped onto the boat and lowered the items he carried before turning toward her and holding up both hands. The moment she moved close enough, he grasped her waist and lifted her easily but didn't let go once her feet touched the deck.

"I've wanted to tell you all day how beautiful you are."

"Th-thank you." The silvery-gray dress was one of her favorites, with a bell skirt and halter neck that left her back bare.

She shivered as his fingertips skimmed across her skin as he finally released her.

"Follow me."

He plucked up the bottle and glasses once more and then took her hand and led the way up some stairs to the upper part of the boat. Once there, she gasped at the sight of the gorgeous tent resplendent with lights with the houses of "bachelor row" lit up from top to bottom, amazed by the sheer beauty of the reception from their vantage point.

"Uh-huh. I thought you might like that view of your handiwork," he murmured, the words whispered into her ear. "And just so you know, I brought the photographer up here to get some shots for you to use in your brochures and stuff. You'll get them soon."

He had?

The statement reminded Eliza of what Marsali had said about Carter going above and beyond to prove his interest.

The cork popped and Carter poured two very full flutes, giving her one before lifting his.

"To second chances and beautiful women."

A huff of a laugh left her before she could stop it. Really, though? He'd left the toast ambiguous enough that he could've referred to Lincoln and Amelia—or to her. So which was it? "To Amelia and Lincoln," she said softly.

They clinked their glasses before sipping, and Eliza watched from their perch as guests began trickling out of the tent toward the front of the homes, where golf carts waited to transport them back to their cars.

The quiet of the night was broken by the sounds of crickets and frogs, the boat bobbing in the water, the low hum of talking and laughter from the tent. It was spectacularly beautiful, the perfect end to what had been a perfect day.

"So what kind do you want?"

"Pardon?"

Carter stood so close she felt the heat of his body enveloping her, warding off the chill of the breeze off the water.

"Wedding. How do you envision your perfect wedding?"

Chapter 18

Asking a woman what kind of wedding she wanted wasn't normally something he did, but for Eliza and her profession, it just came naturally.

At least, until she put her head back and laughed.

"Oh, no way. If I'm ever crazy enough to get married, I'd elope."

He braced his forearms against the railing in front of him, taken aback by her words. "You're joking."

"Nope. What, you don't believe me?"

"I'm just… surprised," he said, his gaze lowering to her lips as they always did when she said the *P* sound that way. Did she do it on purpose? Sometimes he wondered, because it drove him crazy and made him want to kiss her.

Eliza sipped from her glass, her lips damp from

champagne, and lifted one beautiful bare shoulder in a shrug.

Of all of the assets a woman had, he'd never considered shoulders or backs sexy, but looking at her in that dress, all he wanted was to touch her, stroke his fingers over her spine, and kiss her like—

"Yeah, well, after planning so many of them and seeing how crazy people get… I'll pass. Besides, I don't think my headset would pair well with a veil, and I'm too much of a control freak to hand it over to someone else. What about you? Did today make you think about your next wedding?"

"It did." Because the entire time he'd stood up there by Lincoln, he'd found his gaze on a certain headset-wearing wedding planner. "I think I'd follow Lincoln's lead, though. Let her pick the details."

"What did you and Piper's mother do?"

He liked that she was comfortable enough with him now to ask whatever she wanted. "We had a little wedding at the courthouse. Just us and Lincoln and Jill, the minister." He watched as Eliza lifted a delicate hand and brushed the hair back from her face.

She wore it up in a messy twist of some sort that made him want to search out the pins and tug her close for a kiss. But to get there probably meant not talking about his ex. "Now that you have a weekend free of weddings, how about we take the boat out tomorrow for that dinner?"

He saw the way her teeth sank into her lower lip and noted the flash of indecision that crossed her face. His gut tightened as he waited to see if she'd turn him down. Just when he was about to give her his reasons why she shouldn't, she nodded.

"Okay. Yeah, I— That sounds fun."

"Good. Now that that's settled," he said, taking her glass and setting both aside, "dance with me."

"Dance? Carter, I have to get back."

"One dance," he said, taking her into his arms and holding her close. "To celebrate the day."

Carter began to sway to the distant sound of the DJ still playing beneath the tent. Seconds passed, but she didn't relax against him. Couldn't.

"Don't be afraid of me, Eliza."

"I'm not."

"No?" He ran his hand up her bare back, gently massaging as he went, and her head dropped to his chest. From his vantage point, he saw her lips part as she sucked in a breath. "You're tight as a drum."

"S-Stressful job, remember?"

He continued the light massage, loving the way she leaned more heavily against him and tried to hide her gasps of pleasure with every stroke. By the time he made it up to her neck and shoulder, he could feel her melting into him. Was she sensitive to kisses there, too?

Drawn by the scent and feel of her, he lowered his head, letting his lips and chin graze against her temple, cheek, and jawline. She tilted her head and gave him access, and he kissed that place where neck and shoulder met. The caress earned a shiver and low, moaning gasp.

Definitely not as immune to him as she wanted him to think.

Carter opened his mouth and lightly tasted her salty skin again before lifting his head to find her mouth, taking her lips with a slow, heady kiss that promised everything he wanted to give her.

Her responses to him were everything. He felt her hesitation, her inexperience?

Even her fear.

He fought against everything inside of him that wanted to sweep her up and carry her away and forced himself to go slow. Her trembling response tugged at his heart and brought out a protectiveness in him he didn't ever remember feeling, one he couldn't deny.

He gently pressed his thumb under her chin and took her mouth again, deepening the kiss until his head filled with the taste of her. Champagne and chocolate and sweetness, something undeniably Eliza. By the time he ended the kiss, they both breathed heavily. "I have waited an eternity to do that," he whispered against her lips.

She laughed softly, her gaze heavy-lidded as she glanced up at him before lowering her lashes once more and inhaling a shaky breath.

"Two weeks is hardly an eternity."

"Maybe not but it felt like it. Eliza—"

"I-I should go. I'm working, Carter."

Right. She was. And so long as that was her reason for leaving, he'd accept it. "Okay. Yeah, let's go back."

He took her hand in his and raised it to his mouth, brushing his lips over her knuckles. Carter recognized the wariness and panic in her eyes and hoped he hadn't moved too soon. She'd seemed to enjoy the kiss and hadn't pushed him away, though.

That was a good first step.

One he intended to use to climb to the next.

"DON'T GO HOME. STAY HERE."

Eliza looked up in shocked surprise two hours later. The DJ was gone, the tent had been taken down and stuffed into the back of a box truck, and catering loaded the last of their items at this very moment. "Excuse me?"

"I don't mean it like that."

"It sounded like it."

Carter shot her a look of patient frustration.

"It's late. You're tired and we're going out tomorrow on the boat, which means coming back here in the morning so… why not just crash here? Marsali is staying at Mac's. You should, too."

Now that he'd clarified his statement, she breathed a little easier. "I'm pretty sure if Mac was okay with me staying at his place, he would've invited me."

Carter ran a hand over his face and groaned.

"Maybe I'm more exhausted than I thought, because I'm not saying this right. I'm offering you a bed, Eliza. No strings. You can sleep in the house in my spare bedroom or… sleep on the boat if you like."

"We can sleep on the boat?" Marsali asked, sliding deftly into the conversation with a smile and a raised eyebrow at Eliza.

"Yeah. Of course."

Eliza faltered. "Uh—"

"Don't you normally get a hotel room when events end this late?" Carter asked.

Yeah, she did but Carolina Cove wasn't *that* big, so she'd figured she'd just drive the ten minutes it would take to get home. "I don't live far from here," she reminded him.

"Come on, Lizzie, it'll be like all of those sleepovers we had as teenagers. Please? Stay!"

Eliza stared at Marsali. "You do mean sleep, though, right? I hate to sound old but it's been a long day."

Marsali laughed, the sound a little high-pitched.

"Of course. We can girl chat until we fall asleep."

Which, given Marsali's energy at the moment, could take a while.

Mac joined them, a bottle of water in his hand rather than the scotch he'd been drinking earlier.

"What's going on here?" he asked.

"The ladies are going to sleep over on the boat so no one has to drive home."

Eliza watched as Mac lifted a thick, inquisitive eyebrow, just like his sister had done seconds ago.

"You're welcome at my place, Eliza. I have more than enough spares," Mac said.

Eliza split her attention between the men, sensing the tension exchanged in the look they shared. She knew Mac took it upon himself to watch out for her as he always had Marsali, but after that awkward kiss… "Thanks, but—"

"Boat, boat, boat, boat, boat," Marsali said, hands clasped in a pleading gesture.

Eliza laughed. "And how much have we had to drink tonight?"

"Hey, do you know how rarely I get invited to weddings? People want to hire the matchmaker but rarely will they admit using my excellent skills when things work out."

Having heard Marsali issue the same complaint several times before, Eliza sighed. "Fine. We'll stay on the boat."

"Yes!" Marsali cried, hands shooting up in triumph.

Eliza laughed at her friend's champagne-induced antics, but truthfully, she could use a little girl time. She could always sleep later. Especially with it being an otherwise wedding-free weekend. Besides, she needed a scoop on the latest with Marsali and her secret crush, because Eliza had watched Marsali and Oliver talk and dance the entire evening before he'd taken his leave due to him being scheduled to film first thing in the morning.

"So what's left to do?" Carter asked. "How can we help?"

She looked around to survey the area and shrugged. "I think it's done."

Marsali clapped softly and cheered. "Let's go swimming!"

An hour later, Marsali had finally lost her buzz and now floated in the pool hugging Piper's unicorn blowup.

Her friend had left extra clothing in Mac's spare bedroom for convenience, including bathing suits, and while she and Marsali varied in height, thankfully they wore about the same size.

Carter had changed clothes and checked on Piper, who was spending the night with her college-age cousin at Lincoln's. Lincoln and Amelia had changed out of their wedding finery and left to board the private jet—a gift from one of Amelia's Hollywood contacts—carrying them to Aruba for their honeymoon.

Now the group had made themselves at home in Lincoln's pool, and Eliza had to admit the swim had woken up her tired body and refreshed her.

While the guys talked in low tones on the opposite end of the pool, Eliza had her arms looped over a noodle and floated alongside Marsali. "So… you and Oliver looked cozy."

Her bestie had the biggest crush on one of Mac's college buddies ever since Mac had brought him home that very first time so many years ago. But once a picture of the gorgeous Oliver Beck had gone viral, he'd been a star on the rise, first as a model and then an actor. The cameras loved him as well as the general population. Oliver was a guy's guy in personality—and a woman's fantasy with his looks. On the big screen, it was the perfect combo.

Marsali shook her head. "He'll only ever be a friend. You know that. But he did say he'll come back to town next month for Mom and Dad's anniversary party."

"But you're still talking? Texting?"

"Yeah. Just like always."

Marsali's disgruntlement with being friend-zoned was tangible, and Eliza knew it was difficult, especially considering Marsali's profession. Finding love matches for everyone but not herself had to suck. "If it's meant to happen, it will. Right?" Eliza asked. "Isn't that what you've told me in the past?"

"Yeah." Marsali straightened and slid closer to Eliza. "And since *my* love life isn't likely to make a change any time soon, let's talk about yours."

"I don't have a love life."

"But you're going out with Carter. Tomorrow, I believe he said?"

As though sensing he was the topic of their conversation, Carter met Eliza's gaze from across the pool. The below-water lights lit his gorgeous face—and the wink he gave her—and it was then she remembered that sound carried over water and he probably listened to every word. "We are. To discuss business."

"That's a start. Just follow my rules of engagement and let things flow."

"Rules of engagement?" Eliza asked.

"You *still* haven't read the advance copy I gave you?"

She winced, knowing she was caught in a trap of her own making. "I'm *sorry*."

"As you should be. I would be upset but I know how crazy busy the last few months have been for you since I gave that to you."

"It has been crazy," she said, thinking of all of the networking events and bridal shows she'd gone to on the days when she didn't have weddings scheduled. She'd even taken promo packs around to all of the bridal-wear stores within a decent driving range to introduce herself and make a personal connection with the staff. "I'll read it soon. I promise."

"No worries. The rules are in chapter four."

"Any chance I can get the CliffsNotes?"

Marsali rolled her eyes but just as quickly smiled at Eliza.

"Take things *slow* because it takes time to get to know someone," Marsali said, holding up a finger. "Allow yourself to be *vulnerable* yet brutally *honest* about relationship expectations," she said, adding another finger. "No sleeping together until there is verbal *commitment* of some sort—the likes of which are a personal and moral choice, but important to know ahead of time, before things ever get to that point. Take time to *learn* the other person's love language, personal likes and see if those things work with your own or clash. And," she said, "know your *goals,_dreams, and boundaries* and discuss how they will impact each of you and what compromises will have to be made and agree on who will make them."

By the time Marsali had finished, Eliza's head whirled with questions and fear and more than a little panic. "That's chapter four?"

"That's the first few pages of chapter four," Marsali corrected.

"Wow. Okay," she said softly. "Now I understand why dating is so difficult. That's a lot to consider."

"They're hard conversations to have, but the relationships that last do the work."

Eliza glanced across the expanse of the pool and found Carter's gaze still on her. He'd been listening, she could tell. And in that moment, she was inordinately glad he was.

Paired with his friendship—vetting—with Mac, she felt some of her hesitation in allowing things to get personal with him shift, a good thing considering the kiss they'd shared earlier. But if Carter was willing to open himself up and do the things Marsali had just mentioned…

Holding Carter's gaze, Eliza felt herself dive off the cliff and free-fall into whatever tomorrow would bring. "What, um, else is in your book?"

Chapter 19

The following morning, Carter bit back a groan the moment Eliza emerged from the sleeping quarters of the boat and he spotted her in the cute little sundress. The dress was probably Marsali's, borrowed like the bathing suit last night, but it fit like a glove and he appreciated that fact.

He'd probably come across as sexist if he voiced his thoughts aloud, but he loved it when women wore dresses. Especially when the dress bared Eliza's shoulders and ended above her knees and made her look all kinds of beautiful. "You look great."

"Thank you. I didn't know when you wanted to leave so… Marsali let me borrow this."

"It's perfect." She was perfect. "Before we leave, do we need to swing by your place and get the designs you wanted me to look at?"

The reminder that this was a business meeting

was more for himself than anything. After giving in to the temptation to kiss her last night, the plan was to rein himself in and play it cool. Well, as cool as he possibly could looking at her in that dress—and Marsali's bikini last night. The image of Eliza in that two-piece would be seared in his brain for all eternity.

"No, I've been compiling them in a binder. It was in my car. I got it this morning," she said, a lift of her hand indicating the black zippered notebook nearby.

He smiled at her readiness, wishing some of it would rub off when it came to being a single dad of a precocious mermaid.

"Marsali will be up and off in a minute. She's looking for an earring. I told her she could come with us," Eliza said, not quite meeting his gaze. "She's got a good eye for this type of thing and some great ideas."

"But I can't," Marsali said, moving up the steps from below. "I have meetings today myself. Two new clients," she said with a wide smile. "With luck, I'll be able to send them your way for the wedding planning. Carter, thanks for letting me stay. It was fun. I love sleeping on a boat. Just rocks you right to sleep. Well, after all the girl talk."

Eliza smiled and he watched as the two women hugged before Marsali moved toward the dock.

He stretched out a hand to steady her as she disembarked and then got to work, planning on taking things nice and slow up the Intercoastal to give himself plenty of time with Eliza since their busy schedules might prohibit it from happening again any time soon.

Eliza helped him with the ropes before settling herself into the seat beside him as he put the boat into reverse. "You've done that before," he said.

"My dad and uncles all have boats."

"Yeah? What are they like, your family?"

She lifted a delicate hand and tucked a loose tendril behind her ear.

"Oh, they're family." She shrugged. "They're kind of a rowdy bunch."

As far as a description went, that wasn't much to go on. "Your mom and dad… are they together?"

"No. Not since I was a kid. Look," she said, pointing to a long line of pelicans flying in formation barely an inch over the water off to the right.

He got them moving in the right direction and tried to keep the conversation going. "Any siblings?"

"Halfs."

Yeah, a touchy subject apparently. "Where are they? In town? Close by?"

She turned her sunglass-covered face toward his, and Carter faltered. "Gotta talk about something, don't we?" he asked with a smile.

He felt her studying him, even though he couldn't see her beautiful green eyes.

"Four half sibs, two by each parent. Two brothers in Raleigh, one in Jacksonville, and a sister in Shreveport. I stayed with my mom after my parents divorced because my dad cheated and was more interested in his new bride than his kid. Mom eventually remarried, had kids, and then divorced again when I was in high school. I went to stay with my dad during the summer for a bit while the dust settled, but it turned out he was getting a divorce from his third wife, so I came back to Wilmington and spent the rest of the summer and my senior year with Marsali and her parents."

"That sounds… rough. I'm sorry, Eliza."

"It is what it is. Sometimes I'm blown away by the fact I plan weddings given all the divorces and breakups in my life—my other relatives aren't any better in that regard—but then I see the irony of attending all of the weddings over the years."

The words settled home with the weight of an anchor, and he wondered what she'd think of his two failed attempts. He opened his mouth to blurt it out and get it out in the open when Eliza grabbed hold of his arm. He followed her pointing finger and saw dolphins surfacing.

She smiled so big he couldn't bring himself to sour the mood with more talk about divorces. He'd tell her later. If it needed to be told.

The next hour was spent cruising down the waterway toward Wrightsville Beach. He slowed as they approached the restaurant, and once again Eliza moved to help with the ropes.

A guy spotted her and quickly came to pitch in,

and Carter couldn't help but think it was to get a closer look at Eliza.

Boat secured, Carter thanked the man and placed a possessive arm around Eliza's shoulders, and sure enough, the guy took a last look and backed off.

Carter glanced down to find Eliza staring up at him, but given her sunglasses, he wasn't able to read her expression. "Hey, you hungry?"

Chapter 20

After checking in at the hostess stand, they were seated outside by the railings. The restaurant was busy, but not as busy as it typically was during the tourist season.

Eliza sat across from Carter, thankful for the sunglasses that allowed her to discreetly watch his impact on the females nearby. She saw the double takes, the flirtatious smiles they sent in his direction, but she also noted he seemed completely oblivious.

How was that possible?

A waiter brought their drinks and took their order, and as he walked away, Eliza found herself bearing the brunt of Carter's intense gaze. He'd shoved his sunglasses atop his head since they were beneath the restaurant's cover, and his attention fixated entirely on her. She lifted a hand and smoothed it over her hair.

"It's perfect."

She sucked in a soft breath and sank her teeth into her lower lip, hard.

Carter cleared his throat and braced his elbows on the table.

"So, show me those designs."

"Of course." She grabbed the binder she'd carried from the boat and shifted sideways in her seat to place it in the chair beside her. She unlocked the rings and handed him a plastic-encased sheet of paper. "I have a lot of ideas in here, but something I'd very much like to incorporate is water. Fountains, waterfalls, maybe even a stream? Something amazing."

He whistled softly, eyeing the images. "Wouldn't be cheap."

"I realize that. But the clientele I'm going after wouldn't blink at the cost."

He smiled at her, and she felt her breath catch in her throat at the impact. The kiss last night had… rocked her. Her thoughts on Carter, on dating and relationships, everything. Especially when added to Marsali's CliffsNotes from her book. But so long as she was careful, conscious of every slow step…

"You are the only person I know who could pull off a wedding like this," he said. "These are amazing, Eliza."

What was amazing was his support. When she'd mentioned a water element to James a year or so ago, he'd told her she was crazy. "Well, I'm not sure

how many wedding planners you know but...
thanks."

"You're welcome. What else do you have in
there?"

They spent the next fifteen minutes going over
various items and ideas before their food arrived.
Eliza sat forward, too excited to eat. "Do you really
think you can make some of that a reality?"

"It will take some ingenuity to work around the
sites and make it adjustable to wherever you might
need it placed, but yeah. I've got some ideas on how
to make it happen."

"Well, weddings of that nature would require a
year's planning, minimum."

"There could be permits or special licensing
involved, so that's good."

Eliza stared at Carter as he bit into the burger
he'd ordered, his jaw flexing with every bite. "I...
heard you had a visitor last week."

Carter swallowed the bite and nodded.

"Yeah. I did. You don't need to worry about it,
though. I set him straight."

"He had no right to come to your jobsite."

"Agreed. But since I didn't return his calls, he
decided to make a special trip."

Eliza shook her head at Carter's words. James
really was a piece of work. "I'm sorry."

"Don't be. I think your ex is realizing what a
mistake he's made."

"Meaning?"

"He wanted to warn me away from you."

She blinked at the comment. "I thought he tried to *hire* you?"

Carter tilted his head to the side. "He mentioned working together, too. But he was really there to issue a warning."

"Oh, my— He's with Clarissa."

Carter leaned his elbows on the table again and stared at her over his clasped hands. "Does it matter to you if he is or isn't? Are you still hung up on him?"

Matter to her? Hung up on James? The man had tried to destroy her. "No, it doesn't. Not in a romantic sense. Anyone who would stoop so low as to… I see what he was now."

Carter leaned back and picked up his burger. "Good."

Good? That was it? "What did you say to James? When he… said whatever he said?"

Carter hesitated and seemed to be choosing his words carefully.

"I told him that whatever happened between you and me was none of his concern."

"And?" Because she so knew there was more.

"I may have called him stupid for treating you the way he did, and… told him how glad I am that you're free to pursue."

The next question stalled on her lips before she finally forced it out. "Pursue? You just said that to rub James's nose in the mess he's made, right?"

"You sure you want the answer to that?"

She flicked her tongue over her lips to wet them, her stomach a bundle of nerves and lungs barely doing the job as she tried to breathe whilst staring into Carter's slate gaze.

Something had sparked inside of her last night with the kiss they'd exchanged. Something that loosed the tight grip she had on her fear and opened her heart to the possibilities, terrifying though it was. But she and Marsali had talked into the wee hours of the morning, discussing dating dos and don'ts and how to handle the baggage of previous relationships. In Marsali's words, Eliza couldn't hold Carter responsible for something he hadn't done, just because her family—and James— had a history of it. "I'm sure."

Several long seconds passed before he inhaled and sat forward.

"I don't want to say something that'll scare you away."

She didn't want him to, either, but at the same time, she had to know. He'd expressed an interest in her before. She knew that. But she'd brushed it off and shut him down and now… well, she needed to hear it again. Because one of the things most damaged by betrayal was self-confidence, and she had to own that as a flaw. "Tell me anyway."

He inhaled and sat back in his seat, never taking his eyes off of her. "You're beautiful, smart. Gracious. Sweet. But then there are times when your eyes flash a certain way and I see pure orneri-ness," he said with a small grin. "And I want to grab you up and kiss you so you use it on me."

A soft laugh left her, and she felt heat soaring into her cheeks. "I see." And truthfully? She felt the same way about him, wishing at times he'd follow through and overcome her fears by making her forget her senses.

Like the kiss last night did.

"Sweetheart," he said, lowering his voice, "you might not know me well enough *yet*, but I'm a one-woman man."

"It's… hard to trust someone after that's been done to you."

"I know."

"And then I look at you, and I see the way other women look at you—"

"What other women? Because the only one I see is you."

"How's the food? Can I get you anything else?" the waiter asked.

Eliza blinked at the intrusion and shook her head while Carter told the young man that the food was great. Once the waiter walked away, Eliza straightened in her seat. "What about our… busi-ness dealings? If we allow things to get personal, it could mess everything up."

"It could. If we let it. But who says something's going to go wrong?"

The air left her lungs in a gush. "That's unrealistic."

"Every relationship has issues. Arguments. But if the commitment is there, they're just arguments. It doesn't always have to be the end, Eliza."

She lowered her gaze to the grilled salmon salad in front of her and finally picked up her fork. "This looks delicious, doesn't it?"

After lunch, Eliza opened her binder once more and removed another file. "What's this?" Carter asked.

She smiled at him and flipped open the folder. "This is what I have in mind for Piper's birthday party. I wanted to run it by you and get your thoughts."

She laid the sheets out in front of him, and he felt his mouth gape in wonder. "Wow."

"You like it? I'll warn you now that I may go a little overboard with balloons, but they're big impact, and I have so many left over from various events."

"She loves balloons," he said, taking in the personal-size mermaid-scale birthday cake, surrounded by cupcakes with mermaid tails and sprinkles and clamshell cookies with frosting between the two halves along with a pearl candy.

"Since kids are notoriously picky about food, I'm thinking seashell pasta, pizza cutouts of mermaid tails, and baby croissant sandwiches made to look like crabs," she said, pointing to a photo. "Those can be PB and J or plain cheese. And blue punch otherwise known as ocean water for drinks. Best of all, it can be made ahead of time and is kid-friendly."

"This is incredible."

"Oh, good. I was hoping you'd say that," she said, flipping another page. "And there's more."

"More than this?"

"Yeah, well, you said the party will be at Lincoln's because of the pool, so I found a couple of cute games. And a standing cutout I thought you could make for me? Amelia's friend Izzy volunteered to paint it for us."

The cutout featured three spots for little heads positioned above the bodies of two mermaids and a pirate. "Yes. Absolutely. I've got plenty of stuff perfect for that. I can cut it out and have it to you by this evening."

"Great."

He couldn't believe she'd pulled the party ideas together so quickly, especially having worked on Lincoln and Amelia's wedding all last week. "I have an idea. While I'm dropping off the cutout, how about I also bring some of the shelving we discussed? Maybe I could get into those rooms and get started?"

It seemed only fair—and it was a way to spend more time with her as their schedules allowed.

Eliza sank her teeth into her lower lip again before apparently realizing what she did and stopped. He managed to pull his gaze from her mouth and wished she wasn't wearing those sunglasses.

"It's the weekend. I'm sure you have plans. Don't you?"

"I do—with you. If you say it's okay."

"I… Yes, it's okay. After all, it's part of our agreement so… yeah."

Part of their agreement. Did that mean she didn't want to move forward on a personal level? He wanted to ask but his instincts told him to bide his time. "How about dessert? To celebrate our working together on future projects."

Eliza laughed and shook her head. "Not for me. I had more than enough cake last night. You go right ahead, though."

"Nothing is as much fun if you have to do it alone," he said, winking at her and thoroughly enjoying the flush that rose in her cheeks. "Okay, since we're not having dessert, how about we hop back on the boat and go have some fun before we head back?"

MINUTES LATER, they were back on the water. Carter had snagged the check before she could and paid despite her protests that it was a business meeting about *her* business.

As they'd walked out of the restaurant, she spotted a few heads turning toward them and didn't mind Carter's hand riding her shoulder as he walked by her side.

Now they cruised along the Intercoastal, and she spent the time staring at Carter's strong profile instead of the scenery.

She hated the fear that seemed to be lurking just below the surface, because she'd enjoyed their day. They'd talked business and Piper's party details, but she felt they'd also made a deeper connection during the discussion about her family and James. Then again, having known Carter for only two weeks, she couldn't be sure if it was a connection or merely part and parcel of simply learning more about a new acquaintance.

Carter slowed the power motor and steered the boat out of the traffic into one of the many channels leading toward a marina.

"You ready to try it?"

Try it? "You mean pilot this?"

"Why not?"

She'd been on plenty of boats over the years, but she'd never driven one. James had always insisted he be behind the wheel and would go full-speed down the waterway, uncaring of the chaos caused to smaller boats or others. She knew she shouldn't compare the two men but… "Really?"

Carter grinned at her excitement.

"Yeah, really. I wouldn't have asked otherwise. Get over here."

She took position in front of the controls and listened while he showed her what to do and helped get them moving again. And even though he could've moved away at that point, Carter stayed behind her, his hands resting lightly at her waist.

"Just keep it steady. You're doing great."

"Someone's coming up behind us fast," she said. "What do I do?"

He chuckled and the sound warmed her ear.

"Keep tight on the wheel and ride it out."

The wake created by the James-like boat rocked them back and forth several times before the water settled. Carter's grip at her waist tightened, holding her in place and supporting her.

"Great job. You're a natural."

She tilted her head back to glance up at Carter, smiling at the excitement and praise and the beautiful day, but the moment she saw him looking at her, the expression he wore, she felt her heart sputter. Her pulse picked up speed as adrenaline flooded her system, and it had nothing to do with being a novice boater and everything to do with him kissing her. Again.

She waited. Barely daring to breathe while he lowered his head but stopped just shy of her mouth.

"What's it going to be, Eliza? Tell me no if you don't want me to—"

She wasn't sure how she did it but she rose up on her toes and turned and pressed her mouth to his and ended his words, all at the same time. Carter's hand at her back steadied her even as he pulled her tight against him, and she was vaguely aware of the powerful engine slowing once more.

She wound her arms around his neck, felt his growl of pleasure as he took her mouth in a kiss that held nothing back. He tasted good, smelled better, and she lost herself in the sensation of kissing the man who intrigued her so.

A loud horn blasted, startling Eliza so badly she ended the kiss with a yelp of surprise.

The young men aboard the other boat whistled and catcalled and blew kisses to Eliza as they rolled by and yelled for Carter to take her to the bunks below.

Carter's boat rocked side to side in the waves that buffeted them, and she fisted her hands against Carter's chest as her face filled with heat at what the teenagers meant.

Carter didn't comment, but after a moment, he nudged her face up with a hand under her chin.

She shook her head and couldn't look at him. "I'm sorry."

"Sorry?"

His tone drew her gaze to his and she noted his expression. That made her feel even more uncomfortable, especially in light of her thoughts. "I shouldn't have— Especially when I'm not going to — I'm not going downstairs with you, Carter." She inhaled a shaky breath. "*If* we find ourselves together in the future, it has to happen slowly, *naturally*, and if you can't accept—"

"I do."

His big, tender hands framed her face and demanded eye contact before he gave her a look that melted her insides.

"I accept. You set the pace, Eliza. We'll go as slow or as fast as you want. And no always means no. Okay?"

She palmed his forearms and used him for balance as she leaned into him and pressed a short kiss to his lips, this one lighter, softer. "Okay," she whispered. "Now show me what all this boat can do."

Chapter 22

Carter took control of the boat once Eliza got them close to the dock. Within minutes, they were tied up and he held out a hand to help her onto the planking—until she pulled away.

"Um... Maybe we should keep... *this* to ourselves? I mean, for now?"

He didn't like it, but he understood her hesitation given the added pressure going public would probably bring. "Whatever you say."

He walked Eliza to her white van, which was parked in Lincoln and Amelia's driveway. "I'll bring the shelving by in a couple of hours and get started —if that's okay with you?"

"Of course. Are you bringing Piper? I don't want to have her birthday party stuff out for her to see and ruin the surprise."

"Considering the time crunch you have to get

that done, no. I'll get Breanne or one of her friends to babysit," he said.

"Okay. I guess I'll see you there," she said, glancing at Mac's house.

"You feel it, too, huh?"

"That someone's watching us? Oh, yeah," she said with a laugh.

He opened the door to the van and stepped back. "Get going before Mac comes out here and gives us a hard time."

"It could be Marsali. Her meetings were nearby, I think, so she was planning to walk there. But either way, yeah."

Eliza climbed into the vehicle and fastened her seat belt, and he watched as she backed out of the driveway.

He lifted his hand in a wave and turned to go back to his house when Mac's door opened and *both* siblings appeared. Mac stood leaning with his shoulder braced against the doorframe while Marsali practically danced down the stairs toward him. When she reached his side, she slid her arm through his.

"Hello."

He shook his head at her antics. "Something I can do for you?"

"Nope. Quite the opposite in fact. *I* am going to help *you*."

His gaze shifted to Mac's glowering expression,

and Carter had a pretty good idea of the reason behind Mac's ill mood. "I need help?"

Marsali's laughter echoed off of the houses on the narrow street.

"With Eliza? Oh, yes. Yes, you do." She patted his arm. "How do you feel about a little date coaching?"

TURNED OUT, Marsali had some great insights on her best friend. She led him into Mac's long enough to hand over a copy of her new book—pointing out the rules of engagement in chapter four. While Mac glared at Carter and listened to every word, Marsali warned Carter against moving too fast given Eliza's personal history. Time was his friend and he needed to remember that.

Once he'd left Mac's and found a babysitter for Piper, he drove into Wilmington to pick up the shelving. By the time he made it back to Carolina Cove and Eliza's, it was approaching dinnertime.

Which was why he'd made one additional stop and picked up food for them from his favorite restaurant.

Eliza opened the door, and he bit back a grin when it made him realize she'd been watching for him. "Hey. You like Chinese? I brought dinner since it was getting late."

"Love it. But you didn't have to do that."

"I have a feeling you miss way too many meals while you're working," he said, carrying the bags with him as he walked toward her. "Sorry I'm late. It took me a little longer than I thought it would to get a sitter and pick up the shelving."

"No problem. I've been working all afternoon. I'm ready for a break."

"Good. Food first, then."

They settled at her kitchen bar to eat, and he asked about her afternoon.

"Oh, two more couples who left with James have returned," she said with a nod and a blazing smile that lit up her face.

"That's great."

"Right? One of them is an especially large to-do. *And* they paid electronically once I agreed, to make sure I knew they wouldn't be going anywhere else again."

He was glad things were looking up for her after all she'd been through. "That's fantastic."

The topic of conversation changed to how she'd like her storage set up and other general things, and he enjoyed the time. Eliza wasn't just a pretty face, and she had dreams and goals and ideas that drew him to her like a moth to a flame.

They finished dinner and made their way to the storage rooms, and he realized her afternoon had been spent emptying one of them as much as she could to give him space to work and move about.

He got some measurements, and Eliza helped

him unload the shelving from the truck. "Are you sure it's not too heavy for you?" He could carry them easily, but getting them through the door was an issue because of the angle.

"I'm too excited to notice the weight. Let's go."

Within an hour or so, they had all the units he'd been able to bring unloaded, upright, and fastened to the walls. "I can bring more tomorrow. If you're not busy. Otherwise I can bring them in the evenings after work."

"Um, sure. That'd be fine. I'm going somewhere with Marsali in the morning, but I'll be here the rest of the day."

He'd enjoyed their time together, especially since they'd practically spent the whole day together, but taking Marsali's advice into account, he knew he needed to leave. "Okay, sounds like a plan." He watched as her teeth sank into her lower lip, and he stomped down the groan that wanted to erupt at the thoughts it put in his head. "I guess I'll see you tomorrow then."

She nodded and turned toward the door. He followed her down the hallway, managing to keep his gaze on the sway of her long dark hair for the most part.

At her front door, she turned to face him, gazing up at him with her amazing emerald eyes.

"Thank you. Again. I can't wait to get everything organized."

"I'll stay. Help you. If you like." He watched as

her gaze left his and she lifted a hand and placed it on his bicep, over the tattoo.

"You've done enough for the day."

Carter took a step closer, crowding her against the door behind her. Her lips parted and she tilted her head up. That was all the invitation he needed to snag a goodbye kiss that rocked him to his core, despite the fact he kept it light.

Marsali's words of advice repeated themselves in his head, and he used them as a Geiger counter to keep himself under control so as to not scare Eliza.

He lifted his head, stared into her beautiful eyes, and took a step back.

He liked her. Every moment they spent together, he found out more to like. But patience was key, and if that's what Eliza needed to feel safe with him, that's what he'd give her.

Chapter 23

The week passed quickly, and Eliza had spent nearly every evening of it watching Carter create two beautiful storage areas inside of her house.

She and Kellie did the organizing during the day while also working on upcoming events—including Piper's birthday bash—but she found herself looking forward to those evenings more and more.

Even though it scared her how quickly she'd come to like him. A month had passed since that night he'd walked her to her hotel room. A month that now ended with good-night conversations either on the phone or video chat or simply one last sweet text.

Piper's party was the most fun thing Eliza had planned in a very long time. It also made her think it was another business opportunity she needed to be more open to exploring. There were a lot of wealthy families in the Wilmington area who would be happy to pass off the tediousness of a kid's party to someone else.

"Okay?" Kellie asked from nearby.

Eliza looked up at the amazing balloon display that was the backdrop to the cake table and nodded. "Perfect."

Carter had taken Piper out to run some errands so she wouldn't see or hear the setup process at Lincoln's.

Lincoln and Amelia had returned from their honeymoon the day before, and when Eliza and Kellie arrived to set up, the happy couple joined in, along with Mac and Marsali, speeding up the process even more.

But it was Piper's expression when Carter returned with her in tow that opened the last of Eliza's guarded heart. Piper spotted her friends and the mermaid decorations and balloon arch and burst into tears from sheer joy. There wasn't a dry adult eye among the group as they witnessed the pure pleasure on Piper's face as her birthday dream came true.

Watching Carter comfort his thankful daughter broke the last of Eliza's reservations. Selfish men didn't work as hard as he did—or raise a child so sweet.

Eliza stood at the food station trying to get a handle on her thoughts when she felt Carter nearby and turned to find him watching her.

"You are a rock star," he said. "Eliza—"

She held up a hand, still recovering from Piper's teariness and way too on edge where her feelings for him were concerned. "Her response was all the thanks I need. That was too precious for words."

He moved closer and casually draped an arm around her shoulder, pretending to merely stand beside her to look at the food.

"It was—but I still intend to show you how thankful I am later," he murmured, grabbing one of the crabby croissant sandwiches from the stack and sliding her a wink before moving away.

The party lasted several hours, and while Eliza and Kellie kept things moving food and game wise, she noted Carter making a point to introduce himself to the parents who lingered on the sidelines, watching and taking photographs of the fun. Most of the kids had arrived with moms only, but a few couples were in attendance. Still, seeing the moms' reactions to Carter's looks meant tamping down more than a bit of unease at her jealousy. Carter's looks weren't his fault, but with every feminine smile shot in his direction, Eliza reminded herself that his looks were something *she* would have to get used to.

Finally the party drew to a close, and all the mermaids and pirates left for home except for the birthday girl. Piper was now curled up on one of the many lounges surrounding the pool, playing with one of her new toys.

Carter had taken an armload of bags and toys

back to the house, and with the adults otherwise occupied elsewhere, Eliza made her way over to Piper. "Hey, birthday girl. You have one more present," she said, bringing the nylon bag with a mermaid on it from behind her back. "This is from me," she said. "Happy birthday."

Piper sat up and thanked her before reaching for the gift. She pulled the tissue paper out and gasped at the water globe complete with mermaid, seashells, sand, and a pearl. "It's a nightlight and music box, too. I thought you could put it on the table beside your bed."

"I love it," Piper said, awestruck as she held the gift to her chest. "Thank you."

"You're very welcome."

The girl hugged the globe as she surged toward Eliza and gave her the biggest, bestest hug. Eliza returned the embrace with more than a bit of feeling, unable to imagine anyone, much less her mother, walking away from the precious little girl.

"Daddy, look!"

Piper's hug ended as quickly as it had begun, and Eliza turned to find Carter watching them from a ways away.

"What do you have there?" he asked, his long stride closing the distance between them.

Eliza watched as Piper showed her father the gift.

"Wow. That's really pretty, isn't it?" he asked.

"Yes! I'm going to go put it in my room right now so it's there for bedtime."

"Hey, wait a sec. Let's wrap it up so you don't break it on the way," he said, helping Piper place the globe back into the bubble wrap and tissue and back in the bag for easy carrying. "There you go. Breanne's over there. She's going to stay with you tonight for a birthday sleepover before she goes back to school tomorrow."

"Yay! Sleepover!"

Piper took off, her little feet flying and fish-tail costume swiveling with every step, not slowing her down a bit.

"You didn't have to do that, you know. This party was way more than I ever… It was amazing, Eliza."

She smiled and shrugged. "I saw the globe this week after I met with new clients and knew it was perfect. I had to get it."

He glanced around them before taking her hand and tugging her out of sight of anyone inside.

"Yeah, well, I have to do *this*," he said, lowering his head.

Carter took her mouth in a kiss that left her head reeling and her hands clinging to his biceps by the time he lifted his head.

"Lincoln and Amelia mentioned all of us going to Masonboro Island tomorrow on the boats. Will you come with us?"

With them? Like a couple? On a date?

He stroked his thumb over her bottom lip, distracting her even more.

"Um. I don't know."

"Eliza."

She forced herself to look up, and the moment she stared into those dark eyes of his, she knew she'd lost the battle.

"Come with me. Please."

She inhaled and nodded and knew there was no turning back. "Okay."

"Yeah?"

"Yeah."

NO ONE COMMENTED on Eliza's presence the following morning other than to greet her with smiles and hellos as they loaded up the boats and headed out.

A day spent on the water or sand was a day well spent, and Carter loved taking Eliza to the spot on the uninhabited island where he and Lincoln and Linc's twins had dug out a fire pit a few weeks ago to celebrate the twins' graduating high school.

Piper went, too, along with Breanne, who'd decided to stay a little longer to be able to spend the day on the water.

They anchored the boats and played in the shallows, baked in the sun, and rode on a Sea-Doo Mac had picked up sometime that week to add to their adventures since he didn't have a boat. By late afternoon, they had fresh-caught fish and roasted corn—which Eliza ate with gusto while avoiding his amused gaze—and sat in their beach chairs, sun-weary but content.

Lincoln and Amelia left first with Breanne in tow, heading back to work in the morning after their time away and so Breanne could get on the road back to her dorm. Mac and Carter took care of the fire and cleanup while Marsali and Eliza packed up what was left, leaving nothing behind but their footprints and some ash.

Now Carter looked out over the bow and spotted his towel-wrapped daughter curled up on Eliza's lap, and his heart twisted at the sight. He'd always heard that kids and pets had instincts about people, and Piper's read that Eliza was trustworthy. He thought so, too. But as Carter steered the group home, he couldn't help but think it had been as near a perfect day as possible, but if that was the case, why was there a knot in his gut because of the way Marsali looked at him? Watched him?

He realized the women were friends, but he'd done nothing shady or questionable.

Carter still pondered the question when they docked and unloaded. Piper asked Eliza to walk her home before she left, and the two now went hand in hand up the planks toward the yard. Mac walked behind him, loaded down with beach chairs to store beneath his house.

Marsali lingered, which should've been his first clue that he wasn't going to like whatever was going on in that head of hers. "Something wrong?" he finally asked, bracing himself. "You've been giving me the evil eye today."

"I'd say I'm sorry for that but… yeah. There is."

Her tone of voice left him even more wary, and he straightened slowly, facing her. "What's up?"

"I did something. Something you probably aren't going to like but… I do it on all my clients."

His gaze narrowed. "I'm not your client."

"Even more reason for you not to like it," she said softly.

He crossed his arms over his chest and waited her out.

"When it was obvious you and Eliza were getting close, I did what I always do when it comes to protecting someone I love."

He bit back the curse that sprang to his lips, wondering if there would ever come a time when his past wouldn't haunt him. "You did a background check. Without my permission," he all but growled. "Do I want to know how you got my info to perform the check?"

Marsali tucked her hands into the back pockets of her shorts and lifted her chin. "It's surprisingly easy. The point is, it's obvious that you haven't told Eliza, and since *I know* that *you know* honesty in a relationship—*especially* with her— is *every*thing, I want to know why."

Chapter 24

The following Thursday evening, Eliza stood in the newly organized spare bedroom and basked in the thrill being organized gave her. The shelving was complete in this room and now layered with carefully labeled clear plastic bins.

She took a photo on her phone and sent it to Carter along with yet another thank-you and kissy face emoji. The second room was a work in progress, but since they'd used up all of the free shelving in this room, Carter had come up with an inexpensive plan for the second storage room she couldn't wait to get into place.

She'd seen him on Tuesday evening, when he'd asked her to join him for a walk on the beach. They'd met near sunset and strolled holding hands along the edge of the surf.

He'd been surprisingly quiet, and she'd deduced it to be from a difficult day at work. He was a busy man, after all, and raising his daughter alone, and she knew how exhausted she usually was on a normal day without the added stresses Carter carried as a single dad.

Still, ever since the day they'd gone to Masonboro Island, she'd felt a tension in Carter. But then, she also felt that way with Marsali, which was totally weird, so maybe she was just being too sensitive? Truthfully, she was on edge, because with Carter's absence, she'd discovered something about herself.

She wanted more.

They shared chemistry, yes, but this feeling—this *emptiness*—was more than that. She found herself craving his presence in her home, at her side. In her life. And that wasn't something she'd experienced with James. Oh, she'd looked forward to seeing him, but… she didn't *miss* James the way she missed Carter.

But then, Carter's silence weighed on her. As did the fact he wasn't pushing for more, so maybe his interest had run its course?

Was that it? Was that why he'd been so distant this week?

Was she feeling one way while he felt… another?

Her doorbell rang and she inhaled, determined to have that talk Marsali's book said they needed to have about goals and plans and expectations.

She flipped the light off as she left the room and

hurried down the hallway, bracing herself for the impact Carter always had on her.

She unlocked the door and swung it wide, only to gasp.

"James? What are you doing here?" One look at his bloodshot eyes and ruddy face told her he'd been drinking. A lot. "Did you *drive* here?"

"Walked from the bar," he said, lifting his hands toward her. "Eliza, I never should've done it. I shouldn't have—"

"Stop," she said, shaking her head and bracing her body behind the door in case he tried to bully his way in. "You need to get an Uber and go home."

"No. Eliza, hear me out. I'm *sorry*."

"Okay, you're sorry. Good night, James."

"Wait—"

His hand shot out when she tried to close the door and stopped it. "Let go."

"Just talk to me. Don't you owe me that much?"

Owe him? Seriously? "We have nothing to left to say to one another."

"You're wrong. I have plenty to say. I was stupid, okay? I believed her when she said she loved me. I believed her when she said you just used me and—"

"Wait. *I* used *you*?" Eliza asked, engaging in the conversation before she could stop herself.

"I know. That's what I'm saying. I was stupid. I realize that now."

"Good for you," Eliza said. "I'm glad you real-ized that."

"Baby, don't be that way. I made a mistake. I did and I admit it. Please, let me come back. Eliza, take me back."

A laugh escaped her before she could squelch it, and she shook her head, noting with no small amount of alarm and relief that Carter approached her driveway in his Jeep. "You need to leave. Now."

James groaned and began to cry. He really was a sloppy drunk.

"I have nothing to go home to. They're suing me, all because of her. She took the money but it doesn't matter because I'm—"

A moron?

"—on the contracts. She screwed me over and disappeared with some— She's gone."

"Yeah, well, welcome to the screwed-over club. How's it feel?" Eliza said as Carter parked and got out of the truck with a thunderous expression.

"What's happening here?" Carter said, approaching them and positioning himself so that he stood between her and James.

"James was just leaving."

James shook his head, muttering under his breath about how he'd been done wrong. By Clarissa. And now by Eliza because she wouldn't listen.

"I'll call you a cab," Carter offered.

James cursed Carter and turned away but then

staggered as he spun toward Eliza once more. "Really, Lizzie? Him? You make me sick."

"Watch it," Carter warned.

"Weren't you the one who always said you'd never date someone who racked up divorces like your parents?"

Divorces? What? Her gaze shifted to Carter and she waited for him to speak. To defend himself. Correct James. But he didn't. "James, you know nothing about Carter's life," she said. "If you're angry with me, be angry with me, but leave Carter and his family out of it."

James muttered more curses and stumbled his way toward the road. "Just like your family," he said, laughing and wagging a finger at her. "You'll be sorry you turned me down. You'll see."

CARTER STARED at Eliza's pale face and frozen expression and kicked himself for not taking Marsali's advice and coming clean about his past sooner. He'd told Marsali he wanted to, planned to, but needed to find the right time. And that night on the beach during their walk… he'd tried so hard to work up the courage, but every time he'd opened his mouth, he just couldn't do it. Now time had run out and Eliza had found out in the worst way possible.

"Come in, please," she said softly, avoiding his

gaze. "I'd rather not risk my neighbors hearing any more of my personal life than they already have."

She left the door open, not waiting to see if he followed her or not.

Carter moved into the interior and shut the door behind him, locking it for safe measure in case James made a reappearance. Considering the man headed toward the main road toward some restaurants, Carter was pretty sure someone would spot his staggering walk and report him. Maybe a night in the drunk tank would do some good. Then again…

Carter turned and followed Eliza into her living room. He stared at her back, willing her to turn. Finally she did.

"What did James mean? Carter, is there something you haven't told me? Have you been married more than once?"

"Yeah." He grimaced and held up two fingers, wishing the sign meant peace instead of failure. He watched as Eliza struggled to contain her upset.

"So after hearing about my family and listening to me and Marsali in the pool talking about honesty in a relationship, you thought the best thing to do is lie to me?"

"I was going to tell you."

"When?" she countered.

"I don't know. Soon. I tried to at the beach but… Eliza, I wanted you to have time to really get to know me first."

She crossed her arms over her chest and glared at him, and Carter decided to own up to his reasons. "You're right. I heard you in the pool. I heard all of the rules and advice. I even read Marsali's book."

"And you still didn't tell me."

He nodded, staring into her eyes and hoping they could see into his soul. "Because I didn't want to lose you. Eliza, I listened to you describe your family and… I panicked. Okay? I've got two strikes against me, and I knew if you found out too soon, you'd never agree to see me again, even though the first time I saw you, I knew…"

"You knew… what?"

"That you were different. That you were the woman I've been searching for all of this time. I just… knew."

A huff left her, a mixture of surprise and disbelief and pain. She turned away from him, giving him her back once more.

"I talked to Lincoln," he said, knowing now that everything had to come out. "He said if I wanted a woman of quality—which you are—I had to bring quality to the table so you'd see *me*, not my past."

She didn't comment.

He stared at her back, every muscle and bone rigid. "I planned to tell you, Eliza. I just wasn't sure of when."

More silence. He raked his hands through his hair and pulled, hard. "You want the dirty details?

Let's do this. My first marriage was when I was eighteen, dumb, and drunk. It was spring break, and I woke up married to a stranger. Thirty days later, it was dissolved by her lawyer daddy and a judge friend. It never should've happened and I'm embarrassed that it did, but I can't change it. As to Piper's mom… you know that one. She left, I didn't."

Eliza turned, arms hugging her front. Her expression killing him because of the pain he'd put there. "Eliza, say something."

"I'm… I don't know what to say. If you'd just been honest with me from the beginning…"

"Yeah? And then what? Now's when you have to be honest and own up to the fact if I'd done that, you would've shut me down and judged me, even more than you already did when you first saw me. My past is rough and I did far more stupid things than smart in those early years. But it's the past, not my present."

"I just need to *think*, Carter."

Carter sucked in a breath at her expression. As badly as he wanted her, and he did, he could see the truth she couldn't hide. The judgment.

He took a step back. Then another. "What's to think about? You've already made up your mind, haven't you?"

"Carter…"

"I'm sorry I didn't tell you and you found out this way. That's on me and I own it. But right now?

Your expression tells me I was kidding myself thinking time with you would help you see the real me."

"Carter...."

"You heard two divorces and automatically judged me unworthy." He watched her struggle to put her thoughts into words and realized nothing she said at this point could change how he felt, that he'd screwed up yet again. "You don't need to say anything, Eliza. It's written on your face."

Chapter 25

By the time the weekend rolled around and Eliza worked the Sunday-afternoon wedding, she felt like a walking zombie. The sleepless, bloodshot, dark-shadowed kind with drool leaking from their mouths.

"Hey, boss, interference to your left."

Kellie's voice filled her ears via the headset, and Eliza quickly set out to flag down and stop the golf cart about to ruin the couple's photo session.

She managed to get the driver of the cart to wait until the photographer finished before sending them on their way.

An older woman stood nearby, glass in hand, watching the beach wedding and antics. Eliza smiled at the woman when she passed by her.

"You look tired, my dear."

As a greeting, it kinda sucked. Eliza pinned a smile to her lips and shrugged. "I'm fine." The *I'm fine* response had been her mantra every waking moment since Carter had left her house.

I'm fine, she'd said to Marsali when they'd gone to dinner to celebrate the official release of Marsali's book—which had hit the bestseller list as of yesterday. Whenever Marsali had tried to discuss Carter, Eliza had shut her friend down and declared the night to be Carter-free.

"You're not fine," the older woman said, her gaze narrowing on Eliza's face with the intensity of a soul-seer.

Maybe it was the level of her fatigue or the sympathy in the woman's eyes, but Eliza's eyes flooded with tears, and no amount of blinking could stop the sudden barrage. She gasped at her unexpected response and froze, unable to move or react.

"Oh, my dear. Here," the woman said, finding and pressing a tissue into Eliza's hand. "Walk with me. Just down here a bit."

The woman took Eliza's hand and led her away from the wedding attendees waiting for the bride and groom to join them at the beachside buffet, back toward the water's edge, where Eliza had stopped the golf cart. "I'm sorry. I don't know why I'm like this."

"Oh, I think you do. Who is he?"

A laugh burst out of her at the insightful question. Crying to laughter? Eliza wondered if she was having a breakdown. "It doesn't matter. He's... gone."

"Because?"

They walked slowly, barely moving, and the words just exploded out of Eliza in a blubbering gush as she explained the situation with Carter to a total stranger with a gently wrinkled face and kind eyes.

"Tell me, has this gentleman given you reason not to trust him?"

"Not... not that I know of."

"So your fears—while genuine—are based on what's happened with your family?"

Eliza nodded. "After he told me, I thought I could handle it but he's right. He said he saw the judgment on my face, but I couldn't help it. He's been married. *Twice.*"

"Honey, I doubt many people go into marriage thinking, oh, I can't wait to get divorced. It sounds as though he was genuinely embarrassed by his past and that's why he didn't want to tell you."

"I know. I think he is but—"

"But?"

"But he's *ended* two marriages already. How do I know he won't end another and I'll be strike number three?"

"Does he seem to be that type of man? One who doesn't take his responsibilities seriously?"

Eliza thought of Carter and his loving relationship with Piper, the way he was with his employees and his business, Lincoln and his family… "N-no, but—"

"Do you not believe he's changed?"

Changed? "I don't know. I hope so. I *think* so. But how would I ever know for sure?"

"That's where faith comes in," the woman said. "Can I share a secret with you?"

Eliza sniffled and blinked at the woman, nodding and laughing at the same time. "Of course. I've just embarrassed myself in front of a guest. Please tell me something that will help me feel better."

"I will then. Do you see that hunk of a man standing over there? Balding, a bit of a belly? Blue suit?"

Eliza smiled at the description and sniffled. "I do."

"Well, that beautiful man is my husband, and between the two of us, we share five marriages."

Eliza sucked in a gasp so sharp it nearly choked her and she coughed. "Oh. I-I'm sorry, I didn't mean to imply—"

"Stop apologizing, dear, and listen. I told you that to say this—life happens. Usually when we least expect it. In Bart's case, alcohol ended his first two marriages. Then he got sober. As to my first husband… well, I was young and stupid myself, and when I couldn't hide the bruises anymore, I decided enough was enough."

Eliza stared at her new friend, hanging on to every word. "And the... fourth?"

A sad smile flickered over the woman's lined face.

"My Arthur passed away a week after we'd wed. Car accident."

"I'm so sorry."

"Me, too. But then," she said, inhaling, "I met Bart. And even though our pasts were full of mistakes, we fell in love. Next month will be our thirty-fifth anniversary."

Eliza inhaled sharply. Thirty-five years? After all of *that*? "That's wonderful."

"It is. And had we not moved beyond our mistakes and fears, we wouldn't be here today celebrating this wonderful day. Everyone makes mistakes of some sort, but it's how we pull ourselves out of them and move forward that matters most. Bart hasn't taken a drink in all of these years and is a changed man. I changed, too, because I found my self-worth, and the brief love I knew with Arthur made me realize I didn't want to spend my life alone. It hasn't been easy, but we are both committed to living our best life with each other."

"That's... I think that's what everyone wants." She certainly did. And when she thought of the next thirty-five years or more, the image of the man beside her took the form of tattooed arms and a blinding smile and sexy whispers in her ear.

"Yes, well, now you must decide. Do you think

your young man has changed from who he once was?"

"He has. I-I think he has."

"Well, then, can you really blame him for wanting you to see the man he is, rather than the one he's embarrassed about? Especially if he knew of your fears? It sounds to me like he wants very much to be the man you need him to be."

"I made him feel less than," she whispered. "How do I fix that? Carter will always think I doubt him now."

"Grandma, we need you in the photos!" someone called.

"Trust runs both ways, my dear. You fix it by proving to him you were taken aback by the news, but you see the man. Now, I have to go. Will you be okay?"

Eliza nodded and hugged the woman, whispering her thanks. The woman walked toward her family and the waiting photographer, and Eliza watched as her balding, older husband met her with a sweet kiss, tucking her beneath a protective arm as they joined the group under the driftwood arbor.

Trembling to the very depths of her soul, Eliza lifted her fingers to her headset and pressed the button to speak. "Kel, I have to leave. Can you handle things here?"

Chapter 26

Carter sat at the bar, sandwiched between Mac and Lincoln. He wasn't sure why Mac had insisted they come here to eat since it was the same hotel where he'd first laid eyes on Eliza. Knowing Mac, it was to torture Carter and rub salt in the wound.

"Marsali said Eliza looks awful," Mac said.

"They make a matched set then," Lincoln added from Carter's left.

He glared at his so-called friend and brother in the mirror over the bar, his drink halfway to his lips when he spotted Eliza crossing the lobby behind them.

Carter swiveled on the seat and glanced at Mac long enough to see his smirk.

"You're not the only one who can read a calendar—or want her to have help if she needs it."

Carter took off out of the bar, his gaze taking in Eliza's small frame. "Eliza."

She swung around and he hated himself when he spotted her red-rimmed eyes. She did look awful—beautiful but gaunt, like she'd lost weight and hadn't slept. "Hey."

Eliza blinked at him, her head shaking slightly as though she tried to clear her vision.

"What are you doing here?"

"Where are you going?"

The questions were asked in unison, filled the space between them and hung there in awkwardness. "The, uh, guys— Mac knew where you'd be and brought us in case you needed help."

"Marsali," she whispered.

He nodded, uncaring about the details. Only that she was there. "Probably. Where are you going?"

"Oh, um, I-I was going up to my room to fix my face before… I was coming to see you."

"Now? Aren't you in the middle of a wedding?" he asked, his entire body tensing at the hope springing to life inside of him.

"Yes, but… I have to talk to you. Can we? Please?"

Now that his temper and frustration had cooled, talking seemed like a really good idea. "Walk you to your room?"

She smiled, the expression on her face revealing that she remembered the night they first met, and he felt it like a punch to his gut.

Carter stepped toward her and clasped her

shoulder in his hand, tucking her to his side, and tried to be the strength she needed looking as tired as she did.

"I'm sorry," she whispered. "You were right about me… about me *judging* you. I totally did that and it was wrong of me and I apologize."

"Apology accepted," he said, stopping in front of the elevators. He punched the button with a finger and waited for her to continue.

"I wish you'd told me the truth from the beginning—"

"Me, too," he readily agreed.

"But I also totally get why you didn't. After what I said about my family, you knew I'd… I'd have a problem with it. That I'd see the divorces rather than *you*."

Another gut punch. He nodded once, holding her gaze and silently willing her to continue.

"Carter, I'll be the first to admit this scares me, but do you think we can start over? With me being less judgy and you understanding I have severe issues that require complete and total honesty, whether I like hearing it or not?"

The elevator doors opened, and he was beyond thankful that they were empty. He tugged her inside and pressed the door close button, not bothering to wait before gently pushed her into the corner of the elevator and kissed her like the starving man he was.

"Is that a yes?" she asked against his lips.

He stared down into her gorgeous green eyes, maintaining contact as he slowly kissed her again. "That's a yes, sweetheart. I apologize for taking off like I did, but when I saw how disappointed you were and it sank in that I'd blown it, I had to get out of there."

She framed his face in her small hands and kissed him again.

"It wasn't disappointment. It was shock and jealousy and anger and... fear that you'd kept it from me. I let it overwhelm me and—"

He kissed her, hard and fast and purposeful, not letting her up for air until she clung to him and sagged against the wall behind her. "From now on, no secrets." He kissed her again. "We communicate." Another kiss. "We fight... and make up," he growled against her lips, kissing her at the same time. "But we figure it out together. You and me."

She stared up at him, tears glistening in her eyes as she nodded.

"You and me."

FOUR MONTHS LATER, Eliza stared down at the sparkling rings on her finger before shifting her gaze toward her almost-husband.

She wore fitted winter-white jeans and a matching sweater paired with boots and a beautiful cashmere coat borrowed from Amelia. The small group of friends gathered by the Carolina Cove

Pier on a bright February afternoon, called at the last minute so no one could make a fuss, though she would admit to picking the date after hearing Amelia's shooting schedule would allow her to attend.

Marsali and Amelia stood beside her, Mac and Lincoln beside Carter. They'd even taken Piper out of school for the afternoon so she wouldn't miss the special event, and given her seashells to toss in lieu of flowers as they made their way to the pilings beneath the pier for the service.

Now Eliza repeated the vows said by the minister and slid the ring on Carter's finger, barely able to breathe. Not from fear but love. She *loved* this man. This gorgeous, make-her-toes-curl, kiss-her-until-her-head-spun man and his beautiful little girl.

And best thing of all?

They loved her just as much. All her crazy. All her insecurities. All her neediness.

Carter loved her just the way she was, and ever since that day in the elevator he'd gone above and beyond to show her he wasn't the man of his past but a man who had grown up and changed and lived every day striving to be better. For her. For Piper. For the future he wanted with them and the life they'd have together.

The minister pronounced them husband and wife, and Carter used his hold on her hands to tug her closer, lowering his head to seal the pledge with a kiss that promised everything and gave her more than she could've ever asked for. A husband, a daughter. A life she couldn't wait to live with her family at her side.

Carter lifted his head and she blinked up at him, dazed and happy and so very glad she'd broken her own rules and allowed Carter into her walls, her heart. Because in the process, he'd shown her that true love healed.

And in this case? His case? The third time was definitely the charm.

Keep reading for an excerpt of THE MATCHMAKER'S SECRET and turn the page for an excerpt of my upcoming novel SEASCAPES AND VEGAS MISTAKES!

Marsali Jones looked in the mirror and gave herself an affirming nod. The outfit she'd chosen screamed business, and so long as she didn't look at her debit account, she wouldn't scream at what she'd paid for it out of her carefully planned monthly budget. Coming across as a professional was a need, not a want. Right?

The low heels, brown slacks, and rose-gold top paired exceedingly well with the Chanel jacket she'd purchased secondhand off of a resale site, and perfected the image she'd worked to achieve over the last eight years. And now that her career was finally—finally!—taking off, well, a little splurge was okay.

"Are you ready, Ms. Jones?"

Marsali nodded and gave herself a final once-over in the mirror before following the headset-wearing associate from the green room to the wings of the nationally televised studio. Her nerves kicked up multiple levels and she inhaled, then counted slowly as she exhaled.

She'd had her doubts about appearing on this particular show because of the host's penchant for drama, but free publicity was free publicity, and she couldn't afford to pay for the exposure this interview would bring. So long as she stayed calm, cool, and collected, nothing could go wrong. Right?

"And now our special guest will give us all the insight we need to date in the twenty-first century," the host said, smiling into the camera. "Please welcome professional matchmaker and author of the bestselling *Good Girl's Guide to Dating*, Marsali Jones!"

Marsali's pulse raced as she crossed the shiny floor, praying all the while she didn't slip in the heels and go tumbling down like a drunken spring-breaker. She shook hands with the host she'd met backstage before the show had begun taping and waved to the audience before taking her appointed seat.

"Wow. Marsali, I have to say, when they said I'd be interviewing a matchmaker, I expected someone much older and dowdy. I didn't expect our match-maker to be so beautiful, did you, audience?"

Marsali smiled and murmured a soft word of

thanks, uncomfortable with the catcalls and whistles from the audience.

"I've been looking forward to this segment all morning, Marsali. I can't wait to hear your recommendations for dating. I'm recently single, as I told you backstage, and I'm ready to jump into things again."

"Thank you, Gwen. I do have suggestions, and I certainly hope I can answer any questions you might have."

"So tell us—if we've been off the dating scene for a while, how do we start? Where do we start?"

"Both of those are easy. Start where you are. A trip to the grocery store, the gym, a walk in the park. So often we have our head down and earbuds in and we don't notice those around us, but there's a lot of potential out there if we pay attention."

"There are some cuties at my gym. Watch out, boys!" Gwen said, earning another audience laugh. "But where else? What about online dating?"

"Personally, I think we need to dial things back a notch. In our world of technology, romance has gotten lost in swipes and ghosting. If there's someone you're interested in, why not phone them and talk to them in person? Make it more personal by asking them for coffee or dinner. But keep the phones tucked away while you have a real conversation and sincerely invest in getting to know them."

"But what about our introverts out there? How

do they strike up a conversation? Or is that where your matchmaking service comes into play?"

"Well, it certainly can come into play. Match-making is an age-old profession, and I'm thrilled to say that Marsali's Matches has a ninety-two-percent success rate."

"Oh, really?" Gwen said, giving the audience a wide smile. "For clarification, you're based here in Wilmington, North Carolina, but you are national?"

"Yes. I have many clients all over the US."

"Tell us how you got into the profession."

Marsali forced herself to inhale so her voice wouldn't reveal the nerves racking her. "Match-making is something I've always had a knack for. I fixed up friends in high school and college, and when I graduated with a business degree and looked at what I wanted to do, it just made sense to stick with something I love."

"How wonderful. The Wilmington area is largely single, is it not?"

"Yes, Wilmington is about sixty percent single mostly due to the colleges, but also because so many flock to the coast when they feel in need of a fresh start, whether it's after a breakup or being widowed or divorced."

"Who hires you? More men or women?"

"It's fairly even, actually. People today have busy lives and work long hours. If they aren't into bars and clubs, which skew to the younger set, they aren't sure where to go to meet people. I help with that and do a bit of investigating before they ever get to the first date."

"Investigating? That sounds interesting! Tell us more."

"Of course. I take my clients' safety seriously, and I run background checks on any potential date as well as my clients so there aren't any surprises, at least on paper. It helps to weed out those with criminal histories, domestic violence charges, or those wanting to date when they're already married."

The audience laughed and Gwen nodded repeatedly.

"Yes, we definitely need *those* weeded out, don't we, ladies and gentlemen? Mm-hmm." Gwen turned to look at Marsali once more. "Marsali, you wrote a book on dating for good girls. Tell us a bit about that."

"I'd love to. I wrote the book when I was actively dating and realized the men I was meeting were mainly looking for hookups and not interested in something more substantial. I was frustrated and began to establish a set of rules or guidelines to use to weed them out. That became the catalyst for the book and ultimately the rules used by Marsali's Matches."

"What kinds of rules are we talking about here?"

"Well, the gentleman always pays for the first date. Always. It may seem sexist, but I found myself on a date once thinking my date would pay or at least split the check, but he had other ideas and I wound up paying the tab."

"Oh-ho! I'd say he didn't get a second date."

"He did not. Though he did ask," Marsali said, smiling. "Another rule is that my clients meet at the location and no home addresses or numbers are exchanged until at least the third date because usually by then you have a better idea of whether or not there's any crazy in the mix that the background check didn't weed out."

Gwen laughed at the news. "What about all these people sending nudes? I take it that's a no-no, too?"

"Absolutely. If that's the kind of relationship you want, that's what you'll get. But if you're looking for something more, something that might potentially lead to the altar, you have to establish boundaries and see them through."

"I see. Well, I can understand that. I'm curious, though. You mentioned coming up with this when you were 'actively dating' and *I* think a matchmaker is only as good as good as her own perfect match. Am I right, audience? I mean, if she can't match herself, how can she accurately match others?"

The dig slid home and Marsali inwardly cringed. Why had she done this again? She felt her face begin to flush at the catcalls and whistles. "Um…"

"Now, now, Marsali. You *have* to give us the

details. Your significant other has to be a gem of a man. I'm guessing tall, dark, and handsome?"

The audience response became even louder, and Marsali felt her entire body break out in sweat. Not the glistening kind but the kind that comes when fear takes hold. "Um… M-my perfect match… is, yes, I suppose he's all of those things."

"Oh? Go on."

Her brain scrambled like the eggs she'd tried to down this morning and couldn't due to nerves. She needed to end this topic. Now. "H-How about we discuss more of the suggestions included in my book?" Surely now the host would take a hint and change the subject?

"Oh, no, girl. You match people for a living. It's only fair you give us a name. Right?" Gwen said to the audience, waving at them to get their agreement. "You're too beautiful to be single. So who is your perfect man? Tell us, what's his name?"

Marsali wanted the floor to open up and swallow her. Was she really not going to be taken seriously because she wasn't attached? "I really can't—"

"*Of course* you can! We have to know who this perfect specimen of manhood is."

"Tell us!" a voice called from the audience.

"Does he have a brother?" asked another.

"Our viewing audience wants to know, girl-friend. Who is the matchmaker's secret?"

The crowd roared, the sound deafening.

This was it. The time to come clean and confess her single status. Her heart raced in her chest, pounding against her ribs, her palms sweaty and slick, the jacket too hot. "I'm not… I-I mean I—"

"Marsali, how can we believe in love when you won't share? You've already said he's tall, dark, and handsome. I'm guessing quite successful, too. Someone special you think of as your perfect match?"

"Oh, well. I-I do, but—"

"And his name is? Come on, sweet girl, we want details. You have to tell us or else how else can we believe in love?"

"Ollie," she blurted softly, and the microphone she wore picked up the breath of sound.

"Ahh, and there we have it," Gwen said, a sly grin forming on her face.

What? Had she really said it out loud? *No, no, no, no!*

"Girl, you should be shouting his name from the rooftops, not whispering," Gwen said. "Especially since Marsali's sweet *Ollie* is short for Hollywood hottie Oliver Beck."

The audience gasped collectively and erupted in applause, shouts, and whistles. The studio audience roared with deafening noise.

"Take a look at this. Our little hometown girl and Oliver Beck are *killing it,*" Gwen said, "as you can see from this picture of the happy couple taken when Oliver was in Wilmington not long ago. How cute are they?"

Marsali looked around until she spotted the image being shown to the audience. The picture was zoomed in and showed her staring up at her brother's best friend with adoring eyes that revealed far too much for comfort. "I— How did you— That was a private gathering." Her parents' anniversary party, in fact.

"Oooh! Girl, we all know when it comes to Hollywood stars, ain't nothing private. Especially when they look like him! So tell us, Marsali, what is it like being Oliver Beck's girlfriend?"

Marsali stared into the blinding lights and stumbled through the next minute of live television looking like a fool with all of her ums, ahs, and silence when Gwen's questions bombarded her.

Obviously they'd kept things on the down low, so were they now going to take things to the next level? Was there a ring involved? Coming soon?

The very moment Gwen gave up trying to coerce another blundering response and the all clear was given, Marsali raced from the set to the ladies' room, gasping for breath when her phone began to ring. She ignored it but it kept ringing and ringing. She fumbled to silence it and groaned when she saw her brother's name appear above her mother's. Her father's. Her best friend, Eliza, who had boarded a cruise ship this morning for her honeymoon. A multitude of unknowns that were rapidly leaving voicemail messages. "Sweet baby Jesus," she said prayerfully, knowing only a higher power could ever deliver her from the mess she'd just created. "What have I done?"

MAKE ME A MATCH SERIES:

- ROMANCE RESET
- RULES OF ENGAGEMENT
- THE MATCHMAKER'S SECRET
- PERFECTLY MISMATCHED
- BY THE BOOK

Prequel: Seascapes and
Vegas Mistakes

THE MEETING

Isabel Shipley smiled at the client who now walked
away with the gallery manager to finish up the
purchase details and smoothed a hand down her
gold sequined cocktail dress. Her feet were killing
her in the six-inch stilettos she wore, but she'd
decided some Vegas glam was definitely in order
when it came to her gallery showcase. The last-
minute invitation might have been insulting to
some, but she'd decided to look at it as an opportunity. That's why she'd scrambled to pack and ship
her work and now stood inside of one of Vegas's
vast hotels greeting locals and visitors alike.

"That looked like a promising transaction."

She turned at the sound of the deep voice and
sucked in a quick breath. She'd noticed the man
immediately when he'd wandered through the

gallery doors, and in the last hour he'd made the rounds, lingering in her section and focusing on her paintings as though they were great works of art. She'd kept an eye on him as he'd studied her paintings, her mind whirling with the need to memorize his lean lines and angles for later, when she was home and able to create. "I believe so."

"Your work is amazing, Ms. Shipley."

Heat flooded into her face, and she blamed the hot spotlights shining down from above, even though they were focused on the art rather than the room. "Thank you. Please, call me Isabel," she said, holding out her hand.

"Everett Drake. Nice to meet you, Isabel. Michael said you were talented but I wasn't sure what to expect."

"Michael?"

"Devoncourt."

"You know my cousin?" she asked.

Everett nodded and held her hand longer than necessary, and she enjoyed the tingle of his touch racing up her arm. Like, seriously, was he for real?

"We're associates. Michael knew I'd be in Vegas this weekend and mentioned you'd be here and why. I'm glad I decided to check it out."

"Me, too. That's so sweet. I…I was told the last night is usually slow, so a friendly face is most welcome."

Oh, was he ever. The man was gorgeous. Tall, dark-haired with just a smattering of gray peeking through at his temples when he turned his head. He wore a dark charcoal suit that appeared tailor-made to fit his body.

"Things look to be wrapping up. I don't suppose you would like to join me for a celebration drink after you're finished here?"

She bit back a girlish *squee* and forced herself to keep her cool. After all, if Michael knew him and told Everett to check her out, well, that alone labeled him as safe. "I'd like that."

"Great. There's a bar next door. I'll wait for you there."

"Okay." Isabel watched him walk away, feeling more than a little wide-eyed at what had just transpired. She fought the urge to fan her face and was glad she hadn't lifted her hand when Everett glanced back at one last time before leaving the gallery, his gaze sliding over her like she wasn't the only one doing some memorizing.

She spent another twenty minutes talking to the gallery curator and saying goodbye to the friend who'd thought to include her when they'd had a cancellation. The remaining paintings would be packed and shipped once the display date was over and sales finalized.

That done, she'd grabbed her bag and ran into the gallery bathroom to freshen her makeup and took a fortifying breath before walking over to where Everett Drake waited.

He stood the moment he caught sight of her

and welcomed her to the table by holding her chair while she settled.

"Are you hungry?" he asked. "I'll treat you to a celebratory dinner."

"No, not really. But, please, feel free to get something if you like."

He smiled at her and she found herself returning the grin.

"I'm fine. Champagne?"

"Oh, yes, please."

He lifted a hand and the waiter immediately appeared with a bottle of Dom. They really were going to celebrate.

She jumped when the waiter popped the cork and flushed when Everett chuckled softly at her response.

The waiter poured two glasses, and once the waiter left, Everett lifted his glass and held it while she matched his movements.

"To your talent and success."

"To new friends," she added.

Everett tipped his head in response to her toast, their gazes locked as they each sipped.

"So, tell me about Isabel."

Even though there was no reason to blush she felt the heat scalding her face. There was just something about him. "I'm an artist," she said, smiling when he did.

"Tell me something no one else knows."

The husky timbre of his voice left shivers racing

over her skin. "I'm…not sure how to answer that. I don't think I know you well enough yet to share those kinds of secrets."

He grinned and dipped his head as though acknowledging her point and poured them another glass.

"What about you? Any secrets you'd like to share?" she asked.

"I've never been to Vegas before."

Oh! Same. Have you gone to any shows? Toured the casinos?"

The next hour was spent drinking the Dom and exchanging stories about miscellaneous things. She discovered Everett was in Vegas to attend his father's wedding, though the news didn't seem to be something he celebrated. Everett also admitted to a secret addiction to old eighties movies from the Gen X era and that led to a debate over the best movie ever.

"You'll never top Princess Bride."

"Hmm. I think I can," she said.

"With?"

"Can't Buy Me Love."

"Ahh, that is a good one," he said with an agreeable nod.

"Patrick Dempsey in his glorious nerdom and pre-heartthrob days."

Once the Dom was gone, Everett leaned forward and brushed his fingertips over her cheek, smoothing her hair away from her face. She noticed his gaze lower and couldn't keep from wetting her lips. His eyes darkened and another shiver shot through her.

"Have you gambled while you've been here?" he asked, changing the subject.

She bit her lower lip and shook her head. "I haven't really had time. And I leave tomorrow so… The answer is no."

He moved his hand into his jacket pocket and removed his wallet, pulling out several bills to pay the tab and tip generously. "There's no time to waste then," Everett said as he got to his feet and held out a hand for her. "What's your pleasure?"

She hadn't spent so much as a quarter in a slot machine so after they left Everett escorted her to an empty one. They played a few rounds, laughing all the while at some of the characters camped out in front of the other machines. From there they tried their hand at blackjack and Izzy was well aware of the admiring looks Everett received from female passersby. Everett had that classic kind of hand-someness found in old black and white movies, the ones where angled jawlines, tailored suits, and quippy damsels in distress were a thing.

After losing several hands to the house, they moved on to roulette.

"Winner gets a kiss," Everett murmured into her ear as he placed several chips on black.

Maybe it was the champagne slowly fading from

her system or the geeky side of Everett that loved old movies, or the fact he seemed just a bit sad and she wanted to make him laugh and remember their Vegas adventure fondly. Whatever it was, she bit her lip and stared up at him as she placed her bet on red.

"Your prize?" he asked.

She pondered the question for a long moment. "If I win, we go to one of those fake wedding chapels to get married and send Michael the photos for a prank," she said, the words leaving her in a gush because she couldn't believe she had the audacity to propose marriage—even a fake one—to someone she barely knew. "He's always pulling pranks with me and my cousins and it's about time I freak him out, if only a little."

Everett's rumbling laugh and gorgeous smile filled her stomach with butterflies and the slow burn of something she couldn't allow herself to acknowledge for fear it wasn't reciprocated.

"Deal."

She shot him what she hoped was a flirtatious glance from beneath her lashes and placed her chips on red. Izzy bit her lower lip, watching as the attendant set the wheel in motion. She found herself holding her breath, hoping beyond hope for the night to get a whole lot more interesting.

Seconds later she gasped out a laugh and turned to bask in her triumph. "Looks like we're goin' to the chapel," she said in a sing-song voice.

It took mere seconds to google the closest fake chapel and head in that direction.

They laughed and flirted on their way out of the casino and when a group of four men stumbled their way too close, Everett wrapped a protective arm around her shoulders and pulled her to his side, shielding her from their drunken revelry. Isabel leaned her head on Everett's shoulder, breathing in his tantalizing cologne and memorizing every detail of this day.

Maybe it was crazy and over the top, but it was her last night in Vegas and she was up for something fun and silly after a week of stress. Especially when it involved the gorgeous man beside her. What woman wouldn't want to fake marry a man like him? And she'd have pics to show for it. Something to remember this wonderful night where her career was finally looking up and she'd snagged the attention of Michael's gorgeous friend who made her pulse flutter and her knees weak.

They made their way through the crowd and down the street to the building, following the map's walking directions until they reached a set of doors. "Here comes the bride and groom," she said.

Everett's smile and the slight shake of his head left her laughing, and she burst into the building the moment he opened the door.

It didn't take long. The chapel had the process down to a science, and within moments, she was tucked into a long white dress, handed silk flowers and a veil, and followed the attendant to the chapel area where Everett waited in a tuxedo that looked a size too small for his tall frame.

The officiant looked like a former Elvis impersonator, but as the photographer clicked away, they took their vows and Everett slid a gaudy, cheesy double-dice ring on her finger before he tugged her close for their wedding kiss. A kiss that seemed to surprise him, too, if his heated expression was anything to go by when he lifted his head.

The second kiss was longer, deeper than the first, and she gasped for air and clarity when the officiant cleared his throat and mentioned others were waiting.

They quickly changed back into their street clothes and gathered the photos and fake marriage certificate from the receptionist. Standing in a corner of the busy lobby, Izzy took a pic of their photo and texted it to Michael.

Mr. and Mrs.!

What???

We got married! When in Vegas…

SERIOUSLY?

Yup. Everett is a great guy! We just decided to go for it. Why not?

Everett's phone buzzed and he removed it from his pocket and chuckled when he saw Michael's name.

They kept the game up for several minutes until

Izzy pushed it too far when she said she and Everett were honeymooning in Morocco. Michael messaged back that he knew better since he had an upcoming meeting with Everett that the man wouldn't dare miss and their prank unraveled from there.

Laughing at their fun and Michael's admission that they'd pranked him, Everett tugged her out the door of the chapel and they returned to the hotel where it had all started. Everett kissed her on the elevator and then walked her back to her room, his arm around her shoulders even though this time there were no drunken strangers making it necessary.

"That was fun," she said outside her room. "Now when we play Never Have I Ever, we can say we've been married in Vegas."

Everett chuckled at her words, and as always, a thrill coursed through her. She liked his deep, rumbling laugh, even though it had sounded a bit rusty at the beginning of the night.

She passed the keycard over the black face above the knob and opened the door to stash her purse and the oversized envelope with their photos and certificate on the hall table. Everett blocked the door and kept it from closing, watching, and she could feel the heat of his gaze on her skin. "It was really nice to meet you, Everett. You made my last night in Vegas the best."

"I feel the same."

She wished she had more nerve, enough to--
"So, um, I have an early flight. I should…"

She watched as Everett's gaze lowered to her lips, and she instinctively flicked her tongue to wet them. A good-night kiss from him would not be a bad thing.

She heard his low groan, the breath leaving her lungs in response as he stepped forward and let the door shut behind him. He gently prodded her back against the wall and lowered his head, pressing his lips to hers.

That kiss…

Everett stole her senses, her mind. Her body. She wrapped her arms around his neck and reveled in the embrace as one kiss blended into many, many more. It was the goodbye she didn't want on a night she didn't want to end.

But her flight left first thing in the morning and she didn't do things like this. Meet men in bars and--

"Isabel…"

Her name was a low growl filled with every ounce of desire and awareness she felt in response to his touch, and she understood the silent question.

Everett raised his head and avoided her kiss and when she felt his fingers gently grasp her chin she forced her lashes up. Stared into his gaze as he searched hers.

That low rumbling growl mixed with a groan made her toes curl. And then he kissed her again.

Be sure to read Isabel and Everett's complete story in Seascapes and Vegas Mistakes as part of the Carolina Cove series!

COMING SOON:

- SEASHELLS AND WEDDING BELLS
- SEA GLASS AND SECOND CHANCES

THE LAST GOODBYE
FAITH AND JUSTICE
WORTH DYING FOR
LOST LOVE FOUND

Books Also Set in Carolina Cove

COMING SOON:

- SEASCAPES AND VEGAS MISTAKES
- SEASHELLS AND WEDDING BELLS
- SEA GLASS AND SECOND CHANCES

MAKE ME A MATCH SERIES:

- ROMANCE RESET
- RULES OF ENGAGEMENT
- THE MATCHMAKER'S SECRET
- PERFECTLY MISMATCHED
- BY THE BOOK

THE SEASIDE SISTERS SERIES:

- THE LAST GOODBYE
- LATTES AND LULLABYES
- MAP OF DREAMS
- WORTH THE RISK
- LOST LOVE FOUND

WANT TO READ OTHER BOOKS SET IN MY FICTIONAL COASTAL TOWN OF CAROLINA COVE? CHECK OUT AN EXCERPT OF THE LAST GOODBYE:

Dominic Dunn hit his turn signal and waited for a family of five to cross the sidewalk before he turned into the Carolina Cove Inn lot and parked, dread filling his stomach. Just the sight of the happy families and tourists wandering the sidewalks, lounging on restaurant patios, and enjoying the lively Saturday night left him angry. He should've ignored the letter. Ignored his next-door neighbor and best friend, ignored his boss and coworkers who said he had to honor Lisa's last request and come here.

"Mister? You gonna get out?"

The boy's voice startled Dominic and he turned to see a kid around eight years old watching him. The salt-air breeze blowing through the open windows of his car brought with it the smell of fried foods from the restaurants nearby, and seagulls squawked as they flew overhead.

"Mister?"

"Yeah," Dominic said, only then realizing he'd

pulled into a parking place and was literally sitting there with his foot on the brake as he debated his choices of whether to throw the new car in reverse and floor it to get out of Carolina Cove as quickly as possible… or stay the prepaid two weeks Lisa had booked for him before her death.

"Doesn't look like it. Are you drunk?"

A rough-sounding chuckle left his chest. "Do you get a lot of drunk people here?"

"Sometimes."

"I see. Well, I'm not drunk. Just trying to decide if I want to stay here."

"Oh. You got a reservation?"

Did the kid ever stop asking questions? A memory formed, that of his son, Elijah, at the same age. "Yeah, I do."

"Then why don't you wanna stay?"

Dominic glanced at the clock and noted the time. If he left now, he'd add another six hours to his drive from Atlanta. Not how he wanted to spend what was left of the day. Maybe he should spend the night and head back to Atlanta first thing in the morning? "You've convinced me. I guess I will stay."

"I'll show you the way to the office."

"Do your parents know you're out here near the street? You're awfully young to be wandering about on your own."

The kid's shoulders squared and he lifted his chin to a defiant angle.

"I'm almost ten."

He looked younger, maybe because of his small stature. "Well, almost ten or not, there are a lot of strangers milling around, and it's not safe for kids these days. Are you visiting?" He sounded like an old man talking about "the good old days" but it was true. What kind of parent just let their kid wander the streets in a beach town full of people, some of whom probably waited on the opportunity to grab a kid and head out of town?

"No. I live here. You coming or not?"

The kid had spunk, Dominic had to give him that.

He rolled up the windows of the Porsche 911, killing the powerful engine with another press of a button. He felt a little conspicuous driving the flashy car, but he had to admit he loved the power. Just like Lisa knew he would.

He opened the door and climbed out of the low vehicle, yet another thing to get used to after driving a family-friendly SUV for so many years.

"Wow. You're tall. My mom is too. I hope I'm tall when I grow up."

Dominic locked the car and fell into step behind the boy. "I see the sign for the office. You can head home if you like."

"No. I need to check in anyway." The kid turned around and walked backward, rolling his eyes in classic kid fashion. "Or my mom will freak out and call the police again."

Again? "Does that happen a lot?"

"Her calling the police or freaking out?"

"Take your pick."

"Yeah."

Yeah to… both? Dom bit back another chuckle. Given the kid's intrepid personality, he probably kept his mom busy.

The kid flipped face-forward and Dom watched as the boy ran up the two steps leading to the office. He yanked open the door.

"Mom! Reservation!"

Dom noted the wide southern porch with its rocking chairs and a few chairs and tables before he followed the kid inside, well able to see why Lisa had liked the inn so much if the porch and office interior were anything by which to judge. It was her style of decorating. Beachy but understated.

The office walls were a soft gray with blue and sand-colored accents. There was a comfortable-looking couch and chair in the waiting area, a rope swing hanging from the ceiling in front of a painted mural of the beach and ocean behind, and on the opposite side, a coffee bar, popcorn machine, and snack area with a couple of parlor-type tables and chairs.

"Mom!"

"Samuel, how many times have I told you? No yelling. Inside voice," a woman stated as she appeared from a hallway behind the chest-high desk.

Dominic stilled, uncomfortable with the stomach-punching fact he found her beautiful. He'd guess her age to be early to mid-thirties, tall like her son said, at around five eight. Her auburn hair was scooped back and held at her nape, but curly tendrils framed her face and highlighted striking eyes that matched the blue of the ocean painting behind the check-in area.

"But, Mom, you have a reservation and sometimes don't hear me."

"A— Oh," she said, locking gazes with Dominic. "Sorry about that. Welcome to Carolina Cove Inn. I'm Ireland Cohen, the manager."

He forced himself to focus on her name rather than her beauty. "Ireland? Like the country?"

"Yes."

"Unusual name."

"Unusual family," she said by way of explanation. She flashed them both a smile. "I hope I didn't keep you waiting too long?"

"Not at all. Samuel kept me company."

"Mom, you should see his cool car! I'll bet it goes really fast. Does it?"

"It does."

"Maybe you'll take me for a ride sometime?"

"Samuel."

"I'm leaving tomorrow."

"Oh."

"And even if he wasn't, Samuel, that's not something you ask our guests. We've talked about this, remember?" the boy's mother said while sliding her son a stern glare.

"Yes, ma'am."

Samuel glanced at Dominic and rolled his eyes, and yet again Dom found himself stifling a chuckle. And wondering at the last time he'd laughed so much in such a short span of time. "Tough break, kid."

"Let's get you checked in. Name?"

"Dominic Dunn."

"Domin—"

His name ended with a gasp and Ireland's eyes filled with tears. She blinked rapidly and managed to keep them from falling, but in that instant, he knew she recognized him—and knew his reason for being there.

CLICK THE LAST GOODBYE TO KEEP READING!

FAQ

Is Carolina Cove a real place?

Carolina Cove is purely fictional; however, it is *loosely* based on one of my favorite places—Kure Beach, North Carolina. Kure Beach is home to a wonderful pier, a pavilion for special events like weddings and birthdays, swings facing the Atlantic, pelicans Pete and George, coffee shops, restaurants, and more. It's also close to the North Carolina Aquarium, Carolina Beach, and Wilmington.

Can I stay at the Carolina Cove Inn?

While Carolina Cove and the Carolina Cove Inn are purely fictional, there are plenty of motels and rentals in the area to enjoy. One of my favorites is the Admirals Quarters. Tell them Kay sent you! :)

The pier is real?

Yes! And it has quite a history. Be sure to check

out the Kure Beach Pier Cam for a view of Kure Beach and the Atlantic.

What about the restaurants and coffee shops and places you've mentioned in the series?

London's Lattes is based on two of my favorite local coffee shops in Kure Beach and Carolina Beach. Are there more? Yes, plenty. But those two shops I know well because I've visited fairly often while writing these stories. Neither of them on their own was perfect for what I had in mind for London's, however, so I basically combined the two and ta-da! London's Lattes was born. But, no, if you go into either of them, you won't find London's exact business. Isn't fiction wonderful?

Why make up a city? Why not use Kure Beach?

One of the best things about writing fiction is that when a story appears a certain way, you can write it just that way. Carolina Cove and the characters appeared to me in story form and while Kure Beach IS one of my favorite places, I had to change some things to better fit the series as well as steer far away from any real-life persons/families for obvious reasons. Doing so, that meant also changing the name of the city, etc. But, that said, you will find a slew of similarities in the fictional city and the real one. :)

Where is the dream catcher mailbox?

Unfortunately the dream catcher mailbox is pure fiction and an idea taken from a "beach mailbox" I visited once many years ago. The dream catcher mailbox first appeared in the SEASIDE SISTERS SERIES.

Update: I have been told a mailbox has been placed at the southern end of Ft. Fisher but I cannot confirm this.

How did you research the matchmaking aspect?

Oh, the answer to this was fun! Wilmington actually has a professional matchmaker. I interviewed her to get my details straight and learned a lot about a very fascinating business!

MAKE ME A MATCH SERIES:

- ROMANCE RESET
- RULES OF ENGAGEMENT
- THE MATCHMAKER'S SECRET
- PERFECTLY MISMATCHED
- BY THE BOOK

THE SEASIDE SISTERS SERIES:

- THE LAST GOODBYE
- LATTES AND LULLABYES
- MAP OF DREAMS
- WORTH THE RISK

- LOST LOVE FOUND

COMING SOON:

- SEASCAPES AND VEGAS MISTAKES
- SEASHELLS AND WEDDING BELLS
- SEA GLASS AND SECOND CHANCES

Also by Kay Lyons

MONTANA SECRETS SERIES:

- HEALING HER COWBOY
- IT HAD TO BE YOU
- HERS TO KEEP
- MILLION DOLLAR STANDOFF
- HIS CHRISTMAS WISH
- THEIR SECRET SON

THE SEASIDE SISTERS SERIES:

- THE LAST GOODBYE
- LATTES AND LULLABYES
- MAP OF DREAMS
- WORTH THE RISK
- LOST LOVE FOUND

TAMING THE TULANES SERIES:

- SMALL TOWN SCANDAL
- THEIR SECRET BARGAIN
- CROSSING THE LINE
- THE NANNY'S SECRET
- SOMEONE TO TRUST

THE STONE RIVER SERIES:

- WORTH THE WAIT
- NOT BY SIGHT
- THROUGH THE VALLEY
- LEAD ME NOT
- CHRISTMAS AT HOLLY WOOD
- THEIR CHRISTMAS MIRACLE
- SECOND CHANCES

SMALL TOWN SCANDALS SERIES:

- BRODY'S REDEMPTION
- FALLING FOR HER BOSS
- WITH THIS MAN

SECRET SANTA SERIES:

- SECRET SANTA
- SECRET SANTA II: A CHRISTMAS TO REMEMBER

MAKE ME A MATCH SERIES:

- ROMANCE RESET
- RULES OF ENGAGEMENT
- THE MATCHMAKER'S SECRET
- PERFECTLY MISMATCHED
- BY THE BOOK

About the Author

Kay Lyons always wanted to be a writer, ever since the age of seven or eight when she copied the pictures out of a Charlie Brown book and rewrote the story because she didn't like the plot. Through the years her stories have changed but one characteristic stayed true— they were all romances. Each and every one of her manuscripts included a love story.

Published in 2005 with Harlequin Enterprises, Kay's first release was a national bestseller. Kay has also been a HOLT Medallion, Book Buyers Best and RITA Award nominee. Look for her most recent novels with Kindred Spirits Publishing.

For more information regarding her work, please visit Kay at the following:

www.kaylyonsauthor.com

@KayLyonsAuthor (Twitter)

Kay Lyons Author (Facebook)

Author_Kay_Lyons (Instagram)

Kay Lyons, Author (Pinterest)

SIGN UP FOR KAY'S NEWSLETTER AND RECEIVE UPDATES ON NEW RELEASES,

CONTESTS, PRE-RELEASE BOOK INFORMATION, EXCLUSIVES AND MORE!